I0596569

Who Says How She Died?
By
Jerry M. Self

jerrymself.com

These stories are works of fiction.
Names, characters, places, and
incidents are either products of the
author's imagination or used
fictitiously. Any resemblance to actual
events, locales, or persons, living or
dead, is entirely coincidental

Cover art by Frederick Breedon

www.musiccityshooter.com

For Maralee
Because I said so

Albuquerque Journal
March 13, 2012
2 Doctors Challenge Assisted Suicide
Law
by Olivier Uyttebrouck

A pair of New Mexico physicians plan
to file a lawsuit this week seeking legal
protection for doctors who help terminally
ill patients die, attorneys said Monday. ...

The lawsuit will ask a judge to clarify a
decades-old New Mexico law that makes it a
felony to assist a suicide ...

Chapter One

Lance looked up from the garden and saw Willow standing in the back door.

"How's it going?" she asked.

"Great year for weeds. Terrible for grass and flowers."

"A La Niña year," she sighed.

"Yeah, whatever that means."

Removing his cap and wiping his brow, he walked toward her. "Something up?"

She picked dead leaves off his denim work shirt. "Just got a call. I hate to tell you, honey, but Zinnia died." She watched his face. "You knew this was ..." She didn't finish.

He frowned briefly and rubbed his face. "Long time coming."

She picked up the frown in return. "Only a couple of weeks."

"But a long time when you weigh the pain rather than count the days."

She stroked his cheek.

"Should you go to the nursing home?"

He turned to look back at the yard fidgeting with his cap. Shook his head.

"No family. Few friends."

"Lots of friends."

"I know."

She gave him a look that said, "Think about it."

"After all hon. I'm a Presbyterian minister not a Catholic priest. She doesn't need last rites."

"She was a favorite of the staff."

He stepped past her to go inside.

"Good point," he mumbled. "They'll want a prayer at least." Entering the bathroom he added, "Once again you save my behind."

Willow smiled as she closed the back door. "You knew you were going all along," she whispered. "I never talk you into anything you haven't already decided to do."

Sticking his head back out into the hall he asked, "You're on call, aren't you?" He nodded his head in answer to his own question. "Means we'll need both cars. Kid's will have to make do with their bikes."

Willow looked up from folding family laundry in the den. "If you're not gone long, we could let Zach drive the SUV."

She heard him laugh over the sound of the shower.

"Right," she shook her head. "Like we can ever plan on how long you will be."

Lance headed east toward Albuquerque's northeast heights focusing on the emaciated image of Zinnia Foster's face, her eyes closing and a tight grimace tugging the corners of her mouth. He wasn't remembering his last visit with her but perhaps the most significant. He shook his head trying to extinguish the memory of her heroic effort to stave off the pain of the cancer that finally had taken her life.

A sports car cut across in front of Lance to exit Paseo del Norte for the entrance ramp south on I-25. The rudeness brought his attention back to his own driving. An announcer's voice came over the car's radio forecasting that the bright Fall Saturday offered a perfect football afternoon for UNM's Lobos. Lance snapped off the sound then smirked at the thought of possibly attending the game. In five years living in the Land of Enchantment they had never attended a college football game - and not many high school football games for that matter. No family in the First Light Presbyterian congregation boasted a football player though there were a few band members. Zach, the Carroll's senior son, played tennis and golf. So Lance and

Willow supported those events. Gayle, their sophomore daughter, played chess and participated in science fair projects. Neither of which required much parent involvement, even though Lance and Willow showed up more often than the other parents did.

Lance found a spot in the nursing home's parking lot and closed down his thoughts about afternoon athletics as he shut off his car's engine. Mi Casa Senior Care, the long term care facility where Zinnia spent the last weeks of her life, a low faux-adobe building, filled most of a block in the northeast heights of Albuquerque, twenty minutes east of the Carroll's home in Rio Rancho. As Lance climbed out of his car he faced the foothills leading up to the Sandia Mountains where a phalanx of communication towers stood guard over the northern peak. Turning to walk toward the building he was struck once again by the view downhill toward the Rio Grande valley and across the narrow strip of green to the desert stretching past Albuquerque's volcano peaks and on past them nearly a hundred miles to Mount Taylor in the west. Some people found the great southwest dull, monotonous, but Lance always got a thrill from the vistas in all directions.

Quickly, though, the image of Zinnia closing her eyes returned. Time to think about the deceased and her care givers, Lance reflected. Zinnia had moved to Albuquerque some forty years ago with her husband. He had come west to work for Sandia Laboratories and provided a good living for them until he died of a stroke maybe a decade past, Lance remembered. Zinnia had taught high school math, developing a deep concern for students who found themselves pregnant and needing to drop out of school. She and Mr. Foster never had children of their own and so after her husband's death she retired from teaching and helped found a benevolent agency to work with pregnant teens. Primarily the agency assisted the girls in earning a GED. Under Zinnia's leadership they taught their clients personal hygiene and nutrition and provided counseling about the choices they would have to make about marriage, single parenting, giving up the baby for adoption or possibly having an abortion.

Inside, at the receptionist's desk, Lucinda Dominguez welcomed Lance. "Do you want to see Miss Zinnia?"

Lance was surprised. "Is she still here?"

"Oh sure. The morts are never in a hurry to come out here."

"Morticians?"

"Yeah. I call 'em morts."

She waved in the direction of Zinnia's room. "Jennifer is probably still with her."

"How's she doing?"

"She'll be all right. But it's kinda hard on her right now. They were close."

"I know."

Lance moved away from the large windows of the reception area and down the hall past colorful paintings of pueblo women and children gathered around hornos, the mud ovens used for baking. It would be good if he could catch Jennifer Garcia in the room with Zinnia. Jennifer was the hospice nurse assigned to Mrs. Foster. She and Willow had worked together as hospice nurses since the Carrolls had arrived in Albuquerque. Because Willow was on call this week-end she should have been the one to respond when the nursing facility knew Zinnia was dying. But Jennifer was her assigned nurse and had probably spent the night here expecting her death possibly sometime this weekend.

On entering the room Lance found Jennifer sitting by the bed, her hand on

Zinnia's arm. She rose and they arm-hugged shoulder-to-shoulder. They stood there, arms on shoulders, wordlessly looking at their friend. Jennifer stood nearly as tall as Lance. Her dark coloring marked her as a likely southwestern native where Lance's brown hair, blue eyes, and somewhat pale complexion said that maybe he wasn't from around here. Blinds were closed on the single window in the room. Two doors, one to the hall, the other to a toilet-lavatory-shower were both closed. What little furniture there was, a bed, a three-drawer chest, and two chairs, one of them a rocker, crowded the room. The muted light and limited space lent an inappropriate-for-the-minute intimate feel to the room.

"Now she's past the pain," said Lance.

Jennifer leaned over and tugged at the sheet.

"I'm supposed to have her already prepared and ready for the morticians but I'm just not ready."

"I understand."

"I just had more attachment to her." She pulled a tissue from her pocket. "You know?"

"Oh yes, I know."

"The cancer ... so much pain. She was so brave."

"I know. I know."

Lance patted her back. "When did she pass?"

"I think about five this morning. I was asleep in that chair and - I don't know why - but I sort of startled awake and realized she was gone."

"So you spent the whole night with her."

"Yes, well not quite." She shook her head. "That was kinda funny."

"Oh?"

"Uhm. Last night she told me she wanted a private prayer time. She told me to leave her alone about half an hour."

"And you did?"

"Right. I walked around a bit. Then when I got back to the room I guess she went to sleep pretty soon. I read for maybe an hour - no, it wasn't that long and then I fell asleep. I was really tired."

"She was alert, communicating last night?"

"Yes, that is, before her prayer time. The cancer ravaged her body and, you know, she worked hard to tolerate the pain so she could stay alert. She didn't want to sleep her life away. Her mind didn't seem to slow down at all; well, except sometimes the pain caused her to say some weird things."

"Such as?"

"Oh, I don't know. Things like her girls needed her to sew a dress ..."

"I didn't know she sewed for her foundation girls."

"She didn't as far as I know."

Jennifer sat and rubbed Zinnia's arm.

"She said she couldn't take the pain much longer. Actually that's not really a weird thing to say. But it is heart breaking. But what is weird was sometime yesterday she told me she was ready to say good-bye. I asked her if she believed the Lord was about ready to take her. She smiled at me and said 'Well, whether He's ready or not, I'm going to leave.' "

"What do you think she meant by that?"

Jennifer remained silent for a moment. "I'm not sure I really want to know," she finally said.

"You got no other explanation?"

"None. And then ..." Jennifer paused and shook her head.

"And then what?"

"Well. She ..." The nurse hiccupped a laugh then looked at Lance. "She told me to go home. When I insisted that wasn't going to happen, that's when she asked for some alone time." Jennifer stared at the wall. "Hmmm," she whispered.

"Something else?"

Jennifer hesitated, thinking. "She was asleep when I got back to the room."

"Did that surprise you?"

She jerked back to Lance's question. "Well, no, obviously not because I had almost forgotten it."

"You've been here with her a long time."

"Yes, I have."

"Need a break?" He raised his eyebrows.

She hesitated, smiled briefly, and nodded. "I'd like to use the ladies and would rather not -" she nodded toward Zinnia's bathroom.

Lance gave her a tight smile. Jennifer hurried out of the room turning toward the front of the building and the reception area.

Lucinda watched as the nurse disappeared in the ladies' room near the entrance to the nursing home. When Jennifer reappeared she turned to start back to Zinnia's room but caught motion in the corner of her eye. Noticing the receptionist's smile she walked over to her desk.

"How are you doing?" Lucinda asked.

"I'm all right. I usually handle the death of my patients better, but I really learned to love Miss Zinnia."

"Everyone did," Lucinda said with a nod.

"She was special."

The two were quiet for a moment then Lucinda touched her lips and shook her head as though an unpleasant thought had intruded.

"Did it seem to you ..." She failed to complete her thought.

"Did it seem what?" asked Jennifer.

"Well I don't know. I just thought maybe she passed rather quickly. You know?"

Jennifer looked out the front door. "No," she said, "not considering the rapidity of the cancer and the constant pain she suffered."

"Oh, really? But she took pain-relievers, quite a few of them didn't she?"

"Right, but after so long they don't do the job anymore." Jennifer looked at the floor, pushed an imaginary spot with her toe. "You know pain alone can kill you, and of course the cancer was just ..." Jennifer grabbed a tissue from the box on the receptionist's desk.

Lucinda tried a different tack, "But didn't she ..." Catching the nurse's distressed expression, she reddened with embarrassment. "I'm sorry. I ..."

"No, no. It's all right. I just. Uh, I think I'll ..." Jennifer pointed back up the hall and then turned away. Lucinda tried to find something on her empty desk that might need her attention. The nurse walked back to Zinnia's room unaware that the receptionist had turned to stare at her retreating back.

When she re-entered the room she found Lance on the other side of the bed looking down at Zinnia. "I'm so glad you came," she told him. He looked up reprising his tight smile.

He waved a hand at the room. "She lived a full, meaningful, active life and look." He shook his head. "This is what she leaves behind. Well, I guess I know as well as anyone that what she leaves behind is in the hearts of hundreds of people she touched." He tapped the top of the bedside table a couple of times, leaned over and straightened a lace doily, pressed the almost-closed drawer completely shut and then walked around the bed to Jennifer.

She smiled at his tidiness. "Again," she said, "I'm so glad you came."

"Me, too," he said. He took her hand, said a brief prayer, and elicited a promise from her to call if she wanted to talk. Then he left the room.

And he walked into a waiting congregation. He recognized wait staff from the cafeteria and a med tech. Lance was overcome with the obvious love these people had developed for Zinnia. "We heard you were here, pastor," someone said. "She was a favorite," said another. Affirmative murmurings followed. For a few minutes the hallway outside Mrs. Foster's room became a prayer chapel.

Chapter Two

The Carrolls lived in a modest home presenting a street view of the door to their single car garage leading the presentation of their house. What you could see of the front door suggested a small home but once inside the house it proved roomy enough for the four of them. The four bedroom home had become two bedrooms and an office on one side of the house with the master bedroom on the other separated from them by a kitchen, small dining area and some living space at one time designated a great room but simply called the den by the Carrolls. Frank, their ten-year-old dachshund, claimed all the rooms as his own. Their house and those surrounding them sat close to the street. What yard space the neighborhood enjoyed was all in their backyards. The Carroll kids were the oldest in the neighborhood. Exactly as one would expect of homes only a block away from an elementary school, a large number of children filled the neighborhood homes.

Lance drove up to the house just as his son Isaac (everyone calls him Zach) bicycled down the driveway. Zach wore white tennis shorts and sneakers. A navy wind breaker flapped over his chest. He had strapped his tennis bag on the rack over the rear tire.

Sticking his head out the window Lance asked, "Wanta take the car?"

"Nah, biking will be a good warm up for practice."

"Tennis practice in the fall?"

"Sure. Coach says golf and tennis compete for time in the spring, so we get in some informal games when we can."

"That explains a Saturday practice."

"Like I said, informal."

"Be glad for you to drive."

"Thanks, Dad, but I'm fine."

Inside the house Lance pulled a soft drink from the refrigerator. Willow appeared from the laundry room and asked what he found at Mi Casa.

"Well they hadn't come to collect Zinnia yet. Jennifer was in with her."

"And how is she."

Lance gave Willow a hug.

"You nurses think you're so tough but you grieve over every loss."

She tweaked his nose. "What would you think of us if we didn't?"

16

Grabbing an arm she pulled him toward the kitchen table. "You ran off without lunch. I've got us some chicken salad on those thin buns you like." She pried the drink bottle from his hand, replacing it in the refrigerator.

"Where's Gayle?"

"She and Nancy went over to Rosita's." She paused, looking out the window. "Or she and Rosita went over to Nancy's."

The two sat down at the kitchen table to chicken salad sandwiches, cantaloupe slices and iced tea.

Willow swatted Lance's elbow off the table.

"Hey, elbows are okay while I'm saying grace."

"All right but not a second longer."

Frank waddled into the room and lay down under the table, conveniently settled in case any food found its way to the floor.

Both of them proved too hungry for much conversation. When Willow got up to clear the table she glanced at the peaceful landscape past their backyard without noticing it. Had she paid better attention she could see the tops of mountain peaks north of Santa Fe - or maybe Los Alamos. She and Lance could never agree on what they were seeing. "So Jenn is grieving. Disproportionately?"

"I think so," Lance said. "But then Zinnia suffered more pain than most of your patients. I think it got to her."

"Yeah, in team meetings she always had more personal things to say about Zinnia than about any other patients she saw."

"Oh, like what?"

"I dunno. Personal stuff. You know what Miss Zinnia was like. Everybody loved her. You would do anything for her."

"Absolutely true."

"Yeah," Willow nodded, "Jennifer told me she put some Buddhist prayer flags up in Zinnia's room."

"I don't remember seeing those."

"Somebody complained they shouldn't be put in a Christian's room."

"That's petty."

"Uh-huh. So Jenn reverted to taking her chocolate."

"I'll bet she enjoyed that."

"She enjoyed the idea. Toward the end she didn't eat sweets or much of anything. She would tell Jennifer, 'You eat it and tell me about it.'"

Lance stood and looked out at the back yard, nodding his head while not seeing the mountains any better than Willow.

The high school tennis courts presented an unglamorous setting for testosterone driven teens. Drab brown dirt and sand surrounded concrete slabs encircled by chain link fences too tall to climb but too short to capture stray lob shots.

Domingo a tall, wiry figure fired a wicked serve to the shorter though equally wiry Zach but Zach was ready. Ready that is until the wind added a mean curve to the ball. Zach dropped his racket throwing his hands in the air.

"How can you fight this wind," he yelled in disgust.

"Wind?" answered Domingo. "What wind? That was my magnificent spin shot."

"Oh, right, spin! The only spin you know is the twist you put on the stories you tell."

Both boys walked to the net.

"I don't see playing anymore," said Zach.

"Yeah, it was fine until the last ten minutes, but this is too much."

The wind could whip across central New Mexico at twenty miles an hour and sometimes gust up to fifty or sixty. If the boys tried to stay much longer they could imagine having their hides ripped right off their bones.

They saw that the other team members were surrendering to the wind as well. The two turned toward the bench to collect their ball cans and other paraphernalia. Rio Rancho sits on the mesa across the Rio Grande west of Albuquerque as part of the great southwest desert. At this moment the boys were beginning to be pelted by the desert sand. Zach grabbed his ball cap and sunglasses attempting to protect his face from the sand blasting.

"I'm thinking I should have taken my dad's offer to drive his car. Biking home isn't going to be much fun in this wind."

"Just a pleasant tropical breeze," said Domingo.

The boys started walking to the bike stand when Domingo looked back and asked, "What's up with Juan and Deloit?"

Zach stopped and looked back.

"I dunno."

Juan and Deloit had been playing as partners in a doubles match two courts over from Zach and Domingo. Juan seemed to be reading his partner the riot act about something. Deloit was taking it head down until Juan threw a hand up in a what's-the-use gesture and stormed off. Deloit snatched his gym bag off the ground and began walking toward the gate where Zach and Domingo were watching.

Domingo swatted Zach's shoulder. "I'm outa here," he said.

"See ya," answered Zach.

Deloit approached head down, unaware Zach waited for him.

"'S-up?" Zach asked.

"Nothin'" Deloit muttered and pushed past him.

Zach fell in step with him. "Didn't look like nothing."

"Just forget it," Deloit said.

"If I can help ..."

Deloit cut him off, "You can't!"

Attaching his bag to a rack on the back of his bike with a bungee cord he threw a leg over the seat and cycled off.

"See ya," muttered Zach.

Behind him he heard boys saying good-byes and turned to face Juan coming toward the bike stand.

"Hey Zach."

"Juan, ¿Cómo estás?"

"No mucho."

"So, what was that about ... with Deloit?"

"Hmmpf!" Juan threw his bag next to his bicycle. "You been on the same court with him lately? With him or against him?"

"No, guess not."

"He is just not here. He misses shots. He loafs. He comes to practice dog-tired." Juan shook his head and then pulled his jacket collar up against the wind. "I don't know what's going on with him but I'm gettin' outa this wind."

With that the boys mounted their bikes and headed different directions home.

Willow had run in to the drug store to grab some allergy relief when she heard her name called and turned to see Dorothy Klepner. Dorothy, a Presbyterian minister's wife, had befriended Willow when they first came to Rio Rancho. Her husband's church just south of Rio Rancho in Albuquerque was the closest other Presbyterian church to First Light Pres.

"I'm so glad I ran into you, Willow. I've been meaning to call."

"Oh, yes, it's good to see you. But, Dorothy I feel so awful. I owe you a call. We haven't talked since, well, I don't know."

Willow was on her way out of the store when Dorothy had stopped her. The two women moved to activate the automatic door and stepped into the sunshine.

"How's the cane business going?" Dorothy asked.

Willow laughed. "I've forgotten all about that."

"Your kids were going to harvest chollo branches."

"That's right, and scrape the stickers off, varnish them and make canes to sell."

"Well. What happened? Sounded like a great idea."

"Oh, I'm sure it was a great idea. But Gayle got stuck one too many times and the idea perished."

"Oh dear, too bad. I certainly enjoyed listening to you describe their excitement."

"Yeah, well one of the problems involved finding chollo cacti not on protected land. Lance suggested growing a cactus garden in the backyard but Frank and I vetoed that."

"Frank?"

"You remember - our dachshund."

23

"Of course. You named your wiener dog Frankfurter. Cute."

"We thought so."

"Listen, Willow, I've got to get home. What say we meet for lunch?"

"Sure. I'd love that."

So it was settled. They agreed to check calendars and call the next afternoon to settle on details.

Rosita held up the sample bear and shrugged. "Why not just stick with the bare bear?"

Nancy frowned. "A bear bear? What's up with that?"

Gayle laughed. "She meant bare - b-a-r-e. An unclothed or undecorated bear."

"I knew what she meant," groused Nancy. "Let's go look at some clothes."

Rosita and Gayle watched Nancy tromp out of the Build-a-Bear Workshop.

"Whew," said Rosita, "She's in a mood."

The girls had wondered along the lower level of Cottonwood Mall, fingered all the clothing at the Gap and then ran into the stuffed bear shop where they imagined different bears modeled after various teachers. Now Nancy led them on to The Limited.

The typical Saturday crowd moved through the sunlit mall. Gayle enjoyed watching the people. Rosita watched for a particular boy and Nancy appeared to be carefully avoiding anyone she might know. Both Gayle and Rosita had items to search for at The Limited - Gayle wanted shorts, Rosita looked for tops, but Nancy, who left Build-a-Bear to look at clothes, was ready to move on almost the instant they stepped inside the store.

"C'mon. We've seen all this stuff."

"We just walked in!"

"It's the same stuff they have at all the other stores."

So, since no one had a serious agenda they were back into the tidal flow passing a store for more mature women and into, then out of, Bath and Body Works.

Gayle pointed across a meandering family to the Radio Shack display. "Now there's Zach's favorite store."

"I thought his favorite was a sporting goods place," said Nancy.

"Yeah, well that too."

"Whoa," laughed Rosita behind them. "Here's where we'll all end up."

Nancy and Gayle turned to see a display of maternity dresses.

Gayle shook her head. "Not for a long ..."

Nancy immediately burst into tears. Her friends stood, dumbfounded until Rosita moved close to her attempting to protect her from curious passersby and Gayle directed them to an escalator.

Chapter Three

Zinnia Borger was the eldest of three the only daughter and only granddaughter of twelve. Born in Hutchinson Kansas in 1938 to Francine and Xavier Borger. Her father served his community as a hardworking pharmacist of sterling character. Zinnia's earliest memory centered on Mickey, the black cocker spaniel puppy that peed on the kitchen linoleum. Francine had spanked Zinnia because she had neglected to let the dog into the backyard. Zinnia had to clean up after Mickey and as soon as she finished she took the dog outside in back of the garage where, in retaliation, she swatted her pet's behind as hard as she could. The dog yelped and whined and licked Zinnia's hand whereupon Zinnia cried and hugged the dog who licked away her tears.

Zinnia had no memory of the tornado that tore through the edge of town except that she knew it killed her father. She also had little memory of her mother moving the family to Wichita where she taught school. Of course she knew nothing of her mother's struggles with finances but she could remember clearly the result of those difficult times. They moved frequently looking for cheaper places to live. For Zinnia this meant breaking into a new social group every two years or so. It also required her to play second mother to her two younger brothers. The one constant in that shifting scene was Gretchen, her friend from junior high, who kept in contact with her through high school. The two girls didn't let changes in neighborhoods separate them. Sometimes Zinnia would bicycle to Gretchen's house on a weekend but more frequently Gretchen did the traveling. Zinnia's home constantly exhibited a bright outlook. Of course her father had died tragically and moving from one small house to another wore on them, but Francine was a strong Midwesterner who knew how to survive. She didn't let her difficulties get her down. Gretchen's mother, on the other hand, was well provided for by her husband and never wanted for basic necessities. But she lived as though parading through a succession of funerals. As a result Gretchen never missed an opportunity to leave the gloomy atmosphere of her house.

One spring day the two girls bought a teen magazine and retreated to Zinnia's bedroom to devour the vital news of their world. Before even opening the magazine Gretchen had to tell Zinnia that she heard that the young singer, Elvis Presley, was in Wichita for an appearance and for some reason the management of the hotel where he stayed needed him to change rooms. This had happened in the middle of the night according to a reliable source Gretchen knew personally. A friend of her friend was in the hotel and had actually seen Elvis in a robe barely covering his underwear. The question now was, would the magazine have a story about it or was this such a deep secret only a few people in the whole universe knew about it. While searching the slick pages for any update on Elvis the phone rang. Gretchen's father wanted to speak to her.

"No, dad," Zinnia listened to her friend say, "I don't know where she is.

"Well she was still home when I left for Zinnia's."

She asked a couple of questions of her father and hung up. When she turned to Zinnia the blood had drained from her face.

"What is it, Gretchen?"

"Her closet is empty. She's taken her clothes."

Gretchen never heard from her mother again. Both she and her father sought counseling and learned at some point that Gretchen's mother was clinically depressed. She had a little money of her own. Not really enough to live on but evidently enough for her to disappear. Reflecting back on the whole experience Zinnia realized Gretchen always blamed her mother for not getting help, for not taking care of herself.

"At the time," she told Lance, "I just agreed with whatever Gretchen decided to believe about her mother. But later I had to think maybe it wasn't her mother's fault. Maybe Gretchen's father or even Gretchen herself should have seen some signs and should have found the help that her mother couldn't get for herself."

"What did you think about Gretchen's mother?" Lance asked.

"You know I rarely saw her. We were more likely to be at my house than Gretchen's. But what little I saw of her - I don't know. She was a quiet, mousey woman. She rarely said more to me than 'Hello.'"

"So maybe someone else should have helped her?"

"Well, maybe someone did. One of the neighbors raised the possibility that she ran off with another man. Nobody much believed that, but I guess it's possible. But back to your point, I believe the first line of help is yourself. Then, if you can't handle your problems on your own, reach out to someone who can help you. That was my mother's example. Take care of it yourself."

With Gayle's help Willow put a ham casserole with fruit salad on the table and sent Gayle to round up the guys. Willow's mother had imprinted on Willow a deep impression that you won a man and kept him happy through his stomach. Following her mother's example she now made a deliberate effort to include Gayle in meal preparations. As a result Gayle showed promise as a cook, possibly someday even a gourmand. Zach had showered and changed to a blue tee and jeans. He was paging though Facebook on his netbook when alerted by Gayle to come eat. Lance edited tomorrow's sermon on a laptop. But both responded quickly to the promise of food. Frank stayed out of the way of the family's feet while they scurried to the table. But after they had found their places he joined them under Gayle's chair.

After blessing the meal Lance asked, "What's happening tonight?"

"As soon as Gayle passes the salad I'm stuffing my face," answered Zach.

"Save room for dessert," said Gayle.

Zach looked up expectantly. "What's for dessert, Mom?"

Willow looked at Gayle. "Don't know. Did you fix a surprise for us, hon?"

"Just wishful thinking."

"Now there's the surprise," Lance said to his daughter. "I thought you had given up desserts and anything in general that contained plural calories."

"Plura ca-ries?" said Zach with a mouth full of casserole.

"Zach!" protested his mother.

Lance pointed his fork at Zach. "Plural. That's any number over one."

"I can eat anything I want just so long as I limit it to one helping," sniffed Gayle as she tugged down on her cream-colored knit pullover emphasizing her trim figure.

When they finished the meal and it was clear there would be no sugary follow-up

Zach began to collect dishes and clear the table.

"Zach?" said his mother. "Something happen at practice? You've been very quiet."

Zach stood balancing plates hoping the silverware wouldn't slide off. "Yeah," he nodded. "Something's going on with Deloit. Don't know what exactly." He managed to swing the plates over the sink so forks and knives clattered against the porcelain.

"Oh, I've heard some talk," said Gayle. "He's missed some classes."

"I didn't know that," said Zach.

Lance stood and stretched. "I don't imagine there's much you can do to help him if you don't know what's going on."

"Well, I asked but he blew me off. Doesn't want to talk about it. So that's it unless he explains what's going on."

Willow stood and motioned for her teen-agers to get on with cleaning up.

Lance raised a hand to claim attention. "Hold on a minute. I've got an announcement."

Zach placed glasses on the kitchen counter and returned to stand behind his chair.

Flashing a huge smile Lance said, "Lindsey Davis called this afternoon. You remember Mr. Davis?"

Zach waved a hand. "He runs that balloon chase business."

"Oh yeah," said Gayle. "He owns a couple of hot-air balloons."

"Right," nodded Lance. "Well, balloon fiesta is around the corner and he offered a proposition."

"He wants us to crew a balloon!" shouted Gayle.

"No way!" said Zach.

"Yes way," laughed Lance.

"What?" said Willow.

"Okay, here's the deal. If we will assist getting his balloon up and go along in the chase vehicle the first Saturday of the fiesta, we can all go up for a ride in his gondola later in the week. Interested?"

For answer Gayle jumped up and down and then she and her brother slapped hands in a vigorous high-five.

"When did this come up?" asked Willow.

"Well, Lindsey suggested it last week. But I didn't say anything because I figured it wasn't anything more than a casual idea. He called me just before supper and made it official."

"Does this mean we'll get to miss school some?" Zach didn't mind school but he was always open to an excuse not to go.

"No, that won't be necessary. Since we'll be the chase crew on a Saturday there's no problem about school there. And the fall break comes the last half of that week, so we can ride on a non-school day."

"What's up with fall break the first week of October?" asked Gayle.

Willow spread her arms. "Rio Rancho schools are coordinating with the Albuquerque Public Schools, and who knows why they do anything."

"There's a perfectly good reason," explained Zach.

"And that is?" said Lance.

"And that is locked in a safe at APS headquarters only available on a need to know basis."

Gayle nodded. "None of us need to know."

"If you two could learn to tap dance ..."

"Yes Dad," said Gayle, "we could go on stage."

Zach rolled his eyes.

Willow smiled at her two teens and then disappeared into the guest bedroom aka parent's study to call Jennifer Garcia. Lance, having dispensed his good news decided to wander out into the backyard to straighten patio furniture that had been knocked about by the wind.

Zach and Gayle set about the task of arranging dishes in the dishwasher.

"I thought Deloit was your friend," said Gayle.

Zach stared out the window over the sink, nodding his head. "He is."

"So how come you're giving up on him so quick."

"I'm not."

"Sure sounds like you are."

"No, really, I'm not. But I don't know what I can do if he pushes me away from him."

"He shoved you?"

"No, not physically. He just made it really clear he didn't want to talk about it."

"What really happened?"

Zach closed the dishwasher, turned it on and twisted to lean against the counter.

"I don't know for sure. I saw him and Juan arguing. Well, actually it looked like Juan was chewing him out. Deloit wasn't

36

saying anything back. Then, when I asked Deloit about it he just huffed off and wouldn't talk. Juan told me that Deloit wasn't pulling his weight." Zach scratched his head. "He didn't really explain anything."

"Well," said Gayle, "obviously Deloit was embarrassed. Maybe he didn't want to talk right then. That doesn't mean he wouldn't talk later."

"Hmmm. I can see that."

Gayle attempted a stern you-better-do-something-about-it look. Zach jumped to attention and saluted. He left the kitchen laughing.

"Somehow my high school years just disappeared." Zinnia chuckled to herself with this memory. "I studied, hung out with Gretchen and studied. ... What did Gretchen and I do? We studied. The result was earning a scholarship. ... Meaning a trip to Europe or at least the Ivy Leagues? Nope. ... I stayed at home and attended Wichita University."

Zinnia paused frequently to catch her breath. She appeared to be healthy enough.

Her color was still good. But her breathing suggested all was not well.

"Wichita State? That's a good school." Lance nodded approvingly.

"It's okay. Didn't become WSU until I finished there."

"Didn't know that."

"Yeah, I just crossed town to go to college but most of it was paid for. Paid for except for the heart breaks and hospital bills."

"Whoa. What was that about?"

"Well I didn't date much or at all in high school and I thought it was time to break loose and find me a man. I hadn't been on campus a week before my roommate set me up with a blind date."

"Ah ha!"

"Don't get too excited. My roommate came from Enid Oklahoma and set me up with a home town buddy. It seems he had seen the two of us together and asked her about me so she arranged the date. ... He was good looking, polite, a business major and bound to be successful at whatever he wanted to do. Mostly I just wanted to see him again. ... We had the obligatory second date and then he just disappeared into other parts of the campus."

"Didn't work out."

"No and it stung. Turns out I didn't know anything about stocks and investments and he wasn't interested in someone who had no business sense. ... So for my freshman year I reverted to my high school persona. The bright side is I maintained my scholarship required grade point average. I also discovered I wanted a dual major in math and education. ... I went back my second year surrendered to the reality that I would be an old maid but not depressed about it. I enjoyed school and had several girlfriends." She smiled at a memory. "We had student passes to the athletic events so I watched all the male athletes even though I didn't date anyone. ... I was barely conscious of the fact that a football player sat across the room from me in a math class. One day I was engrossed in my notes and walked right into him as I was leaving class. I was humiliated but he picked up my books, ... handed them to me and said, 'You want to do that again? I'll stand here in the middle of the door so you can't miss me.' I laughed and forgot my embarrassment. He smiled and walked off. ... I grabbed the nearest girl and asked who he was. She was bug-eyed with incredulity. 'That's Foster she said. 'Next year he'll be all conference.' 'All conference what?' I had to ask. ... 'All conference running back. What's wrong with you Zinnia? I thought you went to the games with us.' 'Well, I do,' I told her, 'but I don't know who any of the players are.' 'Number 17! Wendell Foster. Don't forget.'

"I didn't.

"And he didn't forget me either but I wasn't aware of that for a long time. He often said hello to me but not much more. ... And we didn't have a class together in the spring. But one day, I suppose a week or so before finals week, we ran into each other in the student center and he asked me to go hiking with him."

"Ah, the first date."

"Not really. He asked me to go with a group planning to hike outside of town and back. I went."

"What's to see? Kansas has no mountains, lakes, or canyons."

"You'd be surprised. What I enjoyed - well just north of the campus there's a cemetery. Maybe there are two cemeteries that run together. Anyway we ran around looking at epitaphs and making up stories about the people buried there. We made up hilarious interconnecting stories."

"Such as?"

"I don't remember. I just remember how funny I thought Mr. Foster was."

"You have good memories."

"It was fun and when we got back he invited me to see a movie with him - that was the first date."

"Oh ho, good news."

"Well, big good news and minor bad news."

"How's that?"

"My roommate was not happy. She had her eyes on Mr. Foster but nothing came of that. When I told her I had a date with him she was shocked. ... The next day she told me I would have to find a different roommate next year. That, as you might guess, was not a hardship."

"Didn't you say something about hospital bills? Really? Were there some medical expenses connected with your college years?"

"Oh yes. Nothing like what it is costing me now to die, but, yes there were some hospital bills."

"Tell me."

"It involves Mr. Foster ."

Lance waved at her to continue.

"The summer between our sophomore and junior years we became pen pals. I just wrote small leaflets describing my summer. ... Mr. Foster wrote cautious but interesting letters about his job with a highway crew. We hadn't written love letters but when we got back to the campus I thought we might have. ... I discovered he was taken with me and I was taken with him being taken with me." She contemplated the scene. "A friend observed that I had made a B on an exam and I told her, 'Who cares.' She said, 'Why Zinnia, you're in love.' That really shocked me. Of course it was true but I had never considered it. Suddenly I worried that I might not finish school and never be a school teacher. ... I called Mr. Foster and said we had to meet. I sat him on a bench in the middle of campus and told him he had to become an all-conference running back and I had to become a high school math teacher and so we must restrict how much we saw one another. ... He frowned at me and said, 'I'm okay with the AC running back and I think the teacher part is great, but what's with this restriction on seeing each other?' I blurted out, 'I'm in love with you and that's a problem!'"

Lance laughed. Zinnia shook her finger at him.

"That's exactly what Mr. Foster did. He stood and took my shoulders in his hands and said, "Zinnia, honey, whatever that is, it is not a problem.""

"Great story. But how does it cost hospital bills."

"Oh it doesn't. But we're getting there."

"Hmmm. All right then."

"Mr. Foster had a friend, Gilly, who lived on a ranch near Matfield Green and we spent Thanksgiving up at his home."

"Matfield Green? Where in the world is that?"

"Oh, it's on the way toward Cottonwood Falls."

"That's helpful."

"Do you know where Strong City is?"

"Of course not."

"You'll find it in the Flint Hills, a beautiful part of God's world."

"Uh-huh."

"Anyway he wanted us to see a fish tank on their property and ..."

"Fish tank? An aquarium?"

"No, no, no. A pond. We called them tanks."

"Oh. Didn't know that."

"So, anyway, we were having a good time playing around there when Mr. Foster decided he wanted to drive an old tractor on the place. Gilly was sure it wouldn't run any more but Mr. Foster was determined. ... He got me to sit on the seat telling me what to push or pull but nothing happened. Mr. Foster began to yank on something and pulled the tractor over onto himself. You know he was a very strong young man." She frowned. "The tractor fell over on him with a crash and I fell with it pining my leg underneath. I both heard and felt my leg break and I also heard the breath gush from his lungs. ... Gilly started pushing and tugging on the tractor but he could not move it. Mr. Foster began to spit up blood. I felt like someone had rammed a hot poker up my leg. 'Get help,' I yelled, 'get help.' ... I could see Gilly wasn't accomplishing anything and he seemed too scared to think straight. The pain was about the worst I ever felt, but Mr. Foster probably had a broken rib penetrating his lung. ... I didn't care if I hurt. He had to live. Well, to make a long story short, Gilly brought help. The tractor got moved and we were loaded into the back of a pickup and taken to a clinic. Mr. Foster did have a punctured lung. I had a fractured femur and wore a cast past Christmas."

"Were you left with a limp or any recurring pain?"

"None at all."

"And Foster?"

"Nothing physical, but he was awfully shy around me until, I suppose around Easter."

Albuquerque Journal
December 11, 2013
Right-to-die Case to Start Today
by Scott Sandlin

... Two physicians and a Santa Fe
woman with uterine cancer want a judge to
allow a doctor to prescribe medication to
provide a peaceful death to a terminally ill
patient - without the threat of possible
criminal charges. ...

Chapter Four

A brisk, sunny autumn day greeted worshippers as they filed out of the First Light Presbyterian Church. The building evidenced the congregation's desire to blend in with the New Mexico landscape. A stucco faux-adobe exterior on the large one-story structure might just as easily have been a Catholic mission. The bright primary colors of the parishioners' clothing cheered the scene considerably.

The service having concluded, Lance half listened to "nice little sermon" comments several older ladies graciously bestowed upon him as he stood at the back of the sanctuary. He was more interested in bits of conversation he had picked up between Willow and a man with a scratchy voice. They were behind Lance somewhere in the foyer of the church. The only sure thing about their comments was the distress in Willow's tone. She was bothered about the information she received.

"Liked your joke," said a teen-aged boy.

"Thanks," said Lance. "Glad you enjoyed it." He didn't remember he had told a joke this morning. Maybe he hadn't. Maybe it was just a humorous remark. Lance didn't think it likely that the boy had intended an ironic critique of his sermon.

The last parishioners were finding their cars and the ushers were finishing their chore of picking up left behind orders of worship and straightening hymnals and bibles in the pew racks. Lance returned to the pulpit to retrieve his Bible and then stepped through the door off to the side of the pulpit into his study. The room, small to begin with was crowded with bookshelves on all available walls. The two doors, one from the sanctuary and one from the hall reduced the wall space somewhat. Before he had his robe removed Willow entered through the hallway door closing it behind her.

Lance raised his eyebrows at Willow's scowl.

"I don't like what I just heard," she said.

Lance sat back against the front of his desk. "And what is that?"

"Somebody, I don't know who, is asking the administration of Mi Casa to look into the death of - well," she paused, staring off into space. "Maybe that's not the word. Maybe they are challenging the administration with an investigation. I don't know. I can't remember how he put it." She took a step forward, turned around and then turned back toward Lance.

"This doesn't sound good Lance. There's an accusation that maybe ... I just don't believe it."

"Accusation of what? Don't believe what?"

She looked up at him almost as if she were surprised to see him standing in front of her. "I'm sorry. I'm just stunned and not making sense."

"Sit." Lance waved at a chair. When she fell into one of the study's cushioned conference chairs Lance sat in its mate beside her.

"What's so upsetting?"

"Someone has accused Jennifer of helping Zinnia commit suicide."

"That's not true," Lance said immediately.

"Of course not. It can't be true. Jennifer would never do something like that."

"Who is ... What exactly has been said?"

"Oh," Willow wrung her hands. "I don't know. Apparently there was an empty bottle of pills in a drawer next to her bed. Powerful pain relievers. The bottle was empty."

"So? I'm sure they were prescribed."

"Well, yes. But it was a fairly new prescription and there should have been more pills. And the bottle probably should have been locked up at the nurses' station."

"That's still ... It doesn't implicate Jennifer."

"Maybe. But whoever is behind this wants a study of all the recent deaths at Mi Casa. It could get ugly and very public."

"They won't like that kind of publicity."

"No, no they won't. But what concerns me is the fall-out for the hospice. The general public doesn't understand hospice programs anyway and if the perception circulates that hospice nurses kill their patients - Oh my God, I just don't want to think about it."

"Who told you this? I couldn't see who you were talking to."

"Max Grafton. He stopped by Mi Casa to see if his mother wanted to get away for an hour and attend church this morning. She didn't, but while he was there one of the attendants told him she had overhead some other staff whispering about something they had heard."

Lance snorted. "Gossip! That's what this is. Gossip."

Willow's glare didn't exactly erase Lance's smirk but he did try to straighten himself.

"All right, it may be hearsay but it is very dangerous gossip, if that's what it is."

Lance took her hands. "I see that. It needs to be stopped."

The door to Lance's study swung open revealing Zach followed closely by Gayle.

"We going, or what?" said Zach.

Lance stood. "Head for the car. We're on the way."

He gave Willow a hand as she stood. "We need to check with Jennifer. I wonder if she's heard about this yet."

"Don't know," muttered Willow.

Lance picked up Zinnia's picture of Mr. Foster, inspected it and then replaced it as the only item on the chest. "Even in your apartment, before you moved here, I don't remember any family pictures." He turned to her for an answer. Zinnia had been slightly overweight for her medium height. She had worn her blond hair past her collar. Even in her last years she was an attractive woman, more handsome than pretty. Now she couldn't move the scales to register triple digits. Her thinning white hair was cut short because, as she put it, "It took less energy to comb short hair." She lay quietly with her eyes closed. She had received some pain medication not long before he had entered the room so he would not have been surprised if she had gone to sleep.

"Don't have family pictures except for those of Mr. Foster and me." Her eyes remained closed and her voice was not much above a whisper. Lance had been standing thinking it was time to leave but now he sat. She might have some other comment.

"Going to sleep?"

Slowly she opened her eyes and stared at the ceiling. "Maybe not. The meds lessen the pain but they no longer get rid of it. At times I can't sleep but I can't wake." She turned her head toward him. "In a hurry?"

"Never in a hurry to leave you."

"In two minutes I can tell you everything there is about my family."

"I doubt that."

"Time me."

Lance directed an exaggerated look at his watch.

"My mother was a wonderful, loving mother." Zinnia turned her face back to the ceiling. "But she was a hardworking, no-nonsense Midwesterner. No parties - work, eat, go to bed then get up early. There was a picture of her somewhere. It's gone now. My brothers left home, achieved success - an astro-physicist and a pharmacist like our father. They got married had kids and their wives wrote newsy Christmas letters. No pictures of any of them. Well, rare pictures in their Christmas letters. None I ever kept. I never sent them pictures. We all had our noses down focusing on what was in front of us." She paused and turned her head to look at him. "Well?"

"Well what?"

"How long was that?"

"Oh right! Hmmm, thirty minutes."

She glared up at him. "I wish I had the energy to swat you." She had an easier time talking but appeared to Lance to be very tired.

"How about a wedding picture? Surely the two of you had a big wedding, football star and honors student."

"No not really. We had some pictures, of course. They may have been in a box of giveaways. I don't know. It wasn't a big wedding. Some family and a few friends came. We were married the summer before our senior year and then moved into a small apartment close to campus. So, many of our student friends who might have been there weren't enrolled for the summer term. The senior year was kind of fun but more nose-to-the-grindstone stuff. The apartment was small but still there was more housekeeping to do than I had been used to with a roommate in a dorm room. We were married students and that put us in a whole different circle. Actually we had found a duplex near the campus. I loved that place. The couple on the other side of the duplex were charming. They were in awe of my All Conference Running Back husband and that, in my mind, was what made them charming. But we didn't have a social life. Our circle of friends constricted rather than expanded. For the most part we were just ready to get on with our lives." She coughed and Lance helped her with a glass of water and a straw.

"You okay?"

She nodded.

"Do I need to go?"

She looked up at him and rolled toward him. "Please. Not just yet."

"What did getting-on-with-it mean?"

"Ah, eventually it meant Fort Campbell, Kentucky. Mr. Foster wore shiny new lieutenant bars and an equally shining Bachelor of Science degree so they made him, naturally enough, the assistant manager of the commissary."

"What did he know about retail?"

"Zero. I guess they wanted a blank slate and that's exactly what they got. He spent long hours making out orders to replace what had been sold and then checking what got delivered. Quite often what he ordered and what he received weren't even close."

"So this was what? Groceries, clothing, sporting goods?"

"Take your average big box store, compress it some and militarize it."

"Really?"

"I don't know. I never went there. If we needed something, he brought it home. I was never sure if it came from where he worked or from off base. There were some frustrations but I think he enjoyed his work."

"And you?"

"Luckily I got a teaching position in a small high school near Clarksville, Tennessee."

"Where's that?"

"Between Fort Campbell and Nashville."

"Teaching what?"

"I taught elementary and remedial math to army brats old enough to drive cars and work in after-school jobs."

"How did that go?"

Zinnia grimaced and rolled from her side to her back.

"Eli was sort of my favorite. He wore torn clothing and came to school every day hungry. But he did come to school every day. I led the class through long division but Eli wasn't getting it."

"Long division? And these kids were sixteen or seventeen?"

"Or eighteen and nineteen."

Lance sat back shaking his head.

"Eli went sound asleep during a test. He was worn out from work and his stomach was rumbling."

"There's nothing you can do about that."

"I started making peanut butter and jelly sandwiches and taking them to school. Mr. Foster complained we couldn't afford it. And we couldn't. But did you ever notice my stubborn streak?"

"Yes. And I'm leaving so maybe you will go to sleep."

Lance tried to leave quickly after arriving so as not to fatigue her. But, conversely, he felt his visits strengthened her spirit, so he returned as often as he could.

"Is ballooning dangerous?" Gayle had barely walked into the house when she turned on her father, her eyes wide.

"Whoa," he said, "where did that come from?"

"Just wondering. The last couple of years there have been accidents."

"Compared to how many safe flights?" said Zach. "It's pretty safe."

Danger just was not an adjective Lance would attach to the Balloon Fiesta. It was colorful, festive and a mark of autumn. Tourists by the droves flocked to Albuquerque to take pictures. Lance had seen a brochure somewhere claiming the Balloon Fiesta was the most photographed event - sporting event, outdoor event, something - in America, or maybe the world. He wasn't sure which kind of event but he didn't doubt it was the most photographed something. For a week bookended by two weekends the sky over the Rio Grande valley would fill with multi-colored balloons, most of them the classic round balls but many of them shaped like cartoon characters or commercial icons. Hordes of eager balloon voyeurs found park-and-ride locations and mounted buses to trek to the balloon park where they would spend the day watching balloon launches, buying souvenirs and eating Mexican food. In no other outdoor sporting event could you stand next to the competitors, talk to them, and photograph the event "up close and personal." Laying out the balloons, inflating them and launching the hot-air transporters was all done at the feet - or in your face, if you will - of the fans. Exciting? Exhilarating? Captivating? Yes. But dangerous? No.

The family distributed jackets, purses, Lance's Bible and other paraphernalia around the house and then Willow summoned Gayle and Zach to help prepare lunch.

Lance stepped behind his daughter to rub her shoulders.

"Having second thoughts about going up?"

She smiled up at him. "Not really. I'm excited about it. All of it. I'm looking forward to the chase and the flight. It's just ... well, I'm starting to notice there's a tricky edge to everything we do. Anything can suddenly turn sour in an instant."

Zach looked up from setting plates on the table. "If you fall out of the balloon, remember to land on your head."

"Who asked you?" Gayle snapped. Willow glared at Zach. Lance pressed Gayle's shoulders moving her so she faced away from her brother.

"Okay, okay," Zach raised his arms in surrender. "You're right. It's getting harder to ignore the risk factors in life."

Lance cleared his throat, a signal that everyone should listen for an important statement. Once Zach had followed such a throat-clearing by announcing, "Quiet everyone, the Grand Poobah is about to pontificate." This time all remained silent.

"The Davises," Lance began, "are one of the most experienced ballooning teams in Albuquerque. I can't imagine a safer crew to fly with."

"I wasn't trying to cast any doubt on our adventure," said Gayle. "I was just wondering."

"Here," Willow handed her a bowl. "Put the potatoes on the table."

Later, with the meal finished, the table cleared and the dishwasher filled and engaged in its utensil catharsis, Lance pulled Willow out to the back yard.

"So, are you going to be all right about this gossip issue?"

"No, I don't think so. This is not a good thing and it could get seriously destructive."

"What would that involve?"

Lance pointed at a tree in the neighbor's yard.

"First sign of autumn colors," he noted.

"Well, for starters it could mean all kinds of legal problems for Jennifer: losing her nursing license, losing her job, maybe even jail."

"But she clearly hasn't done anything wrong. That would never happen."

"You know better. The guilty often aren't caught and the innocent aren't always freed."

"Yeah, I know. But not in her case. What else."

"Our hospice could lose both credibility and accreditation. We could be put out of business."

"I see the threat you're describing but I just don't believe gossip can lead to that end."

Willow took his arm and turned him toward her.

"It shouldn't but it still could."

Chapter Five

Lance entered the room quietly. The room was darkened; the blinds shut; a lamp on the table spread a circle of dim light.

"What kind of day have you had?" Lance pulled the chair closer to the bed.

Zinnia turned her head toward him; her eyes slanted a groggy half-mast. "One of the worst," she whispered.

"I won't stay then - unless there's something I can do for you."

She licked her lips. Lance found a wash cloth and moistened her lips.

"I'm s'posed to say, 'Pray for me, pastor. That's the best thing you can do for me.'"

"Well, sure, I'll do that."

"Just be quiet and wait until I finish."

"'Scuse me."

"Prayer is okay, but I prefer you listen rather than talk."

"Much to the surprise of most people I do a credible job of listening."

"You're the best."

"Are you sure you feel like talking?"

"Of course not. I feel like dying. But I haven't completely worked that out yet."

"By that you mean ...?"

"Just listen."

"Yes, ma'am. In a minute." He picked up her glass and left the room. The door had barely closed before he returned with the glass full of ice. He sat, placed a small cube in her mouth and then put both hands behind his ears.

"I want you to know how we got to Albuquerque."

He nodded.

She intended to tell him about their move to Nashville. Foster had used spare time at Fort Campbell to work on a Master's degree part time at Vanderbilt. With his tour of duty finished he taught high school science while enrolled in a doctoral program at Vanderbilt. Zinnia had been able to continue teaching high school math (the good news) but they could only find positions at different schools. She enjoyed her work and thrived but for her husband the doctoral program proved demanding and frustrating for a full time teacher and more than full time student.

She intended to tell Lance more but quickly found herself too weak to talk. She had forgotten she had told him all this when she first came to the New Light church.

Lance said a quiet prayer and left her room replaying the story in his head as he had first heard it.

Foster had thrown a notebook across the room and pounded on the kitchen table where the two of them studied and prepared for classes.

"It's just too much! I can't do this anymore!"

She tried to hug him but he pushed her away, kicked over the dinette chair, and stomped around their small apartment.

"Quit something, then."

He stopped pacing and stared at her.

"What can't you do? Do you want to quit school? Okay, that would save some money and give us time for sightseeing or entertainment."

He continued to stare, a dazed look on his face.

"Do you want to quit teaching? You could put all your energy into finishing your doctorate. We might be able to borrow some more money. I'm not sure but I think it's doable."

For another few minutes he stood there. Then he shook his head, walked to the chair he had sent sailing and righted it, sitting down.

"No, I don't want to quit anything. We are doing what we are doing because we agreed this was what we wanted. I just needed to throw a tantrum and get it out of my system."

"Is that all?"

"No, there's one other thing," he laughed.

"What's that?"

"I needed to be reminded who's the brains of this bunch."

"Obviously that must be the one earning a doctorate at Vanderbilt."

He chuckled, "Not even close."

Lance remembered that a friend of a friend of her husband had contacts with Sandia Labs in Albuquerque and this led to the Fosters' move west.

Willow looked up a questioning glance as Lance came through the door. He shook his head.

The high school cafeteria seemed louder than usual and it was giving Nancy a headache.

"We need to find someplace quieter," she complained.

As Rosita asked her to repeat herself three boys slowly walked behind Gayle, Nancy, and Rosita. They studiously and artistically ignored the girls. After a few steps they realized their ploy was not working. Somehow the targeted chicks had paid no attention to their macho parade. "Weird," commented one of them. "They must be sick," answered one of his companions. "They clearly aren't tuned to what's best for them," said the third.

Gayle made a follow-me gesture and got up to leave. The three gathered the leavings of their lunch and headed for the cleanup area. In the meantime the three boys, who hoped to attract their attention, watched open-mouthed, amazed that the females seemed to have no awareness of their presence. "Unbelievable," muttered one of the boys.

In the hallway Gayle took the lead hurrying toward the gymnasium, which she knew would be empty during the lunch period. Inside Rosita placed Nancy on the third row of the bleachers while she stood in front of her. Gayle sat just below Nancy on the second row.

"How are you feeling?" asked Gayle.

"Oh, I feel just fine," said Nancy. "Maybe it's too early for morning sickness. I have no idea. Of course I've never been pregnant before and don't really know anyone who has. I mean, you know, personally known anyone well enough that she would tell me stuff."

Rosita shrugged, "It probably is different, anyway, for different people."

"Yeah," agreed Gayle. "Any way we sure don't know anything about it."

"Well who ..." Rosita began but Gayle swatted her knee and glared at her. She then turned to Nancy and asked, "Right, who knows about this, besides us? Have you told your mother or anybody?"

"That's not what ..." Again Gayle showed Rosita a fierce expression.

"I haven't told anyone but the two of you. I don't want anyone to know. But I know, sooner or later, it will get out."

"No," said Gayle, nodding agreement. "It can't be a secret for long."

"Well," said Nancy, "I have an aunt who never had children because every time she was pregnant she miscarried."

Rosita sighed, "That is so sad."

Gayle asked, "Is that common among the women in your family?"

"I don't really know. I've never heard anything like that."

"When I took that home health course - whatever it was - Mr. Granger told us miscarriages happen all the time. Sometimes the girl didn't even know she was pregnant."

Gayle looked from Rosita to Nancy. "Is that what you're hoping for?"

"I can't say what I'm hoping for. I'm just in shock. I didn't know this would happen."

Rosita snorted, "Something's missing from your education."

"I know how babies are made," snapped Nancy. "I just didn't think it would ... Well, I guess I just didn't think."

Rosita quickly sat beside her, throwing her arm around Nancy's shoulders. "I didn't mean it."

Gayle heard an increase of foot shuffling and conversation in the hall and jumped up.

"Gotta get to class, girls."

As they moved toward the door to the hall Rosita whispered, "You're not thinking about an abortion are you Nance?" Nancy shuddered. "You can't do that, Nance. You can't do that."

In the hall Nancy turned left for her next class and Rosita and Gayle moved to the right.

"I wanted her to tell us who the guy is," said Rosita.

"I don't," hissed Gayle. "That would just complicate things and I don't want to know."

"You're kidding!"

"Am not!"

"¡Muy loco!" muttered Rosita.

A delivery van whooshed through the intersection obviously ignoring the posted speed limit.

"Glad you didn't step in front of that," exclaimed Zach.

Deloit turned to see who had spoken and then looked back at the traffic signal.

"Today's not a good day to die."

"What day is?"

Deloit snorted. "Right!"

The light turned and the boys moved across the street.

"Headed home?" asked Zach.

"Nah, I'm gonna hang at the mall a while."

"I don't see that. I'd rather be doing something."

"So you've got your dad's protestant work ethic."

"Not so much." After a moment Zach shrugged. "Maybe."

Deloit laughed. "That's not a bad thing. I get it. You don't want to waste your life."

"Like you said, that's not a bad thing."

A girl in a sweater and tight jeans bicycled past them. For a long time neither boy spoke.

"Bikes go by you real quiet like," said Deloit.

"Almost didn't notice her." They laughed.

"Almost," agreed Deloit.

"Talking about wasting a life," Zach began.

"She's getting her exercise."

"I wasn't thinking about her. Okay, I was thinking about her but I'm talking about you."

"Me?"

"Right. What's the deal about tennis practice?"

"What about tennis practice?"

"Juan thinks you're goofing off."

"Yeah, like Juan never had a bad day at tennis. Last year he got skunked when we went to Santa Fe."

Zach groaned. "He wasn't the only one."

"Wasn't our best match."

"That was last year. What about last week?"

They stopped at the next corner. It was time to go their separate ways. Zach stood waiting for Deloit to come up with an answer. Deloit looked down the street, the direction he would turn and then surveyed the ground seeming to focus on a purple sage as though it would furnish a plausible explanation.

"I dunno," he said. "What do you care?" He turned and trudged down the block.

"Deloit ..."

But Deloit waved him off hunching his shoulders.

Zach discovered Gayle had beaten him home and was in the kitchen spreading peanut butter on a rice cake.

"Now is that what dad would call plural calories? Gotta be at least two there."

"One and one half," she smirked.

"More than one. Still plural. Hey I think you're about to rip a seam there."

"What about you? Dawdling around, taking all day to wander home from school."

"Wasn't dawdling. I was talking with Deloit. At least I didn't head to Cottonwood Mall to hang out like he does."

Gayle rinsed her knife and tossed it in the dishwasher.

"Ha, a lot you know."

Zach grabbed an apple off the counter, bit a hunk out of it and leaned on his elbows on the counter.

"What do you know I don't, oh soph-a-moron?"

"Deloit doesn't hang out at the mall. He works there."

"Are you sure? He works there?"

"Positive. I've seen him. At Burger King's. 'You want fries with that?' The whole bit."

"At Burger King?"

"That's what I said."

"Really?"

She batted his forehead with her palm.

"Nothing wrong with my diction. You hard of hearing or something."

"Why wouldn't he tell me that? He didn't say anything about working. He never has said anything about a job."

"Maybe it's something new."

"Okay but I just talked to him not thirty minutes ago."

Zach dropped onto a counter stool bewildered.

"Doesn't make sense," he mumbled.

"He's male," said Gayle. "Testosterone destroys brain cells."

Lance drove into the driveway to discover an open garage door. Willow pulled a couple of grocery bags from her back seat. He parked beside her SUV and hopped out.

"Rare timing to have you open the garage for me."

"The timing was to get you here to carry in the groceries."

"All a matter of perspective."

Inside Lance emptied the bags while Willow put items on shelves or in the refrigerator. Sounds of a soccer ball being thumped drew Lance to the sliding glass door. He waved to the teens and then turned back to his wife.

"So how was your day?"

"Same-ol', same-ol'."

"Sometimes routine trumps exciting."

"Oh, did learn something. Jennifer is out of town. She took a day to go see her sister about something family."

Lance found the mail one of the kids had deposited on a kitchen counter.

"Hmmm, good," he observed.

"Well, that means she probably hasn't heard anything yet about some investigation into Zinnia's death."

Lance looked up. "Oh right. Any further word on that."

"Lots of words. Everyone is buzzing about it. But no new information."

"Has an autopsy been performed?"

"No, and there might not be one. Usually when an elderly person dies in a health care facility there is an assumption that an autopsy is unneeded."

"Yeah, but if someone raises a question like this."

"Only nobody has officially raised a question. So far all we have is scuttlebutt, gossip."

WHAP! The soccer ball slapped the glass door.

"They can't break that door can they?" asked Willow. "That was quite an errant shot."

"That was shoddy defense," said Lance. He threw the door open and yelled, "Grounded for life."

Lance walked across the kitchen and collected the reusable grocery bags they had emptied. "Even if there's nothing to it, you don't want a lot of talk accusing one of your nurses."

"Exactly!"

"So what now? You're waiting for the other shoe to drop? For someone to make it official?"

"Our director called in the nurses this morning and told us to do everything by the book and to listen carefully."

"Well that's business as usual for you."

"For most of us. Fortunately we have a good crew."

Lance waved the reusable bags, "I'll put these back in your car. Will Jennifer be back tomorrow?"

"Should be. I don't know for sure. You really ought to see her when you can."

"I intend to."

One day Zinnia Foster tried to describe to Lance how much Albuquerque had changed since she and Mr. Foster had moved here in 1970. And Albuquerque, not Rio Rancho was where they lived. Both

Zinnia and her husband were math people. She had taken the teaching route finding a position at Sandia High School. He followed a more scientific path leading him to Sandia Labs. Their interests were complimentary and gave them much to share. Both could understand and appreciate the other's interests and experiences. Neither of them was totally nerdy, you have to understand. Actually they discovered early on a deep interest in the people with whom they worked. Zinnia loved her students and Mr. Foster enjoyed bringing home colleagues for meals. Those who were married sometimes found themselves doing couple activities with the Fosters. His unmarried associates quickly fell victim to Zinnia's matchmaking efforts.

Vincent and Victoria Roybal proved to be favorites. Unfortunately Vincent was a life-long smoker and, as you might expect, developed lung cancer. The only thing Zinnia found herself willing to say to Lance about Vincent's last days was the expected, "Nobody should have to die like that."

Mi Casa Memorial Service for Zinnia Foster

The cafeteria at Mi Casa Senior Care had been converted into a worship center. Folding chairs were spaced so that people on walkers or who otherwise had lost the gracefulness of youth could still navigate to a place to sit. As Zinnia's minister Lance had been asked to preside for a service of remembrance. He stepped to a simple podium and the room hushed.

"Welcome to this memorial service for Zinnia Foster. My name is Lance Carroll. I was Mrs. Foster's pastor. Thanks to Ms. Ingersoll for allowing us to have this service and thank you for attending. I will say a few words about Miss Zinnia and do a few preacherly things like praying and then I hope some of you might want to say something about her.

"You may not know she was a sturdy mid-westerner, a Kansas girl. She spent a little time east of the Mississippi in Kentucky and Tennessee before she came to the Land of Enchantment. She was a mentor who helped found and run the Ladies of Charity House. There she helped teen girls who were pregnant. She told me she liked this room. The colors, the furniture, the decor all have the feel of a pueblo. She said to me, 'Of course they have to give you the right meds, good food, and a comfortable bed, but the first thing is to decorate so people feel at home.' So there you are Sally. Miss Zinnia felt at home here."

Chapter Six

Overnight the jet stream bounced south and blew an early winter arctic gale down New Mexico's neck. Lance graciously drove both Carroll teens to school since they complained their systems were not yet ready to cope with frigid temperatures. A block from school Zach asked his dad to let him out because he saw Juan and wanted to catch up with him. Gayle preferred to stay in the warm car a few more minutes.

"Juan's one of the tennis team, isn't he?" asked Gayle's dad.

"Yeah. They're stewing about their buddy Deloit. He seems to be dropping the ball. Not to make a pun or anything."

"Of course. You wouldn't do that."

"No. It's punitive to pun."

"Oh, a quick point, punctual punning."

"Bad, bad, bad. Give it up Dad. I'm the master."

"Okay. You win. But what about Deloit? I saw him play last year. He's got potential."

"Don't know. Ask Zach." Lance had stopped the car and Gayle abruptly ended the conversation by jumping out to join friends. Lance watched in his rear view mirror as Zach and Juan approached, heads together, intensely debating something.

Zach and Juan rushed into the front hall of the school searching for warmth. Zach dropped his backpack on the floor and shook himself out of his Dallas Cowboys coat. "You said he's working at a lumber yard?"

"That's the reason he gave for quitting, right."

"I heard he was working fast food at the mall."

"That too."

"Two jobs?"

"That's why he said he had to quit the team."

"No wonder he's tired all the time."

"Sure. I would be too."

Zach collected his gear and they started down the hall toward their first class.

Juan took up the conversation again. "I also heard he might have to quit school."

"Makes no sense."

"Not to me either."

Zach scratched his head. "Can't be doing drugs. He's working two jobs, going to school and playing tennis. Not well, but doing it. Couldn't keep it up.'

"I have no idea," said Juan. "No idea at all."

♥ ♥ ♥ ♥

Zinnia joined New Light Presbyterian Church in Rio Rancho on the recommendation of one of the women who helped her with her tutoring/mentoring project. When Lance came visiting as a follow-up on her expression of interest in membership she launched into a story to answer his question about her husband. She began with the commonly shared experience of most Americans who watched planes fly into New York skyscrapers. "I was sobbing into the phone telling Mr. Foster there was a second plane and I couldn't understand why he wasn't responding. Then Gladys, his secretary came on the line to tell me something was wrong with Mr. Foster. He suffered a massive stroke it turns out. When I got to the hospital they told me he was in a coma. The doctor couldn't predict whether he would come out of it or not. Actually, I believe he knew full well he wouldn't. Mercifully Mr. Foster didn't linger. He died before a week had gone by."

"And you believe that was merciful?"

81

"Oh, heavens yes, pastor Lance. Those things can go on a horrendously long time." She swept her eyes across the far wall as though searching a bank of memories. "He was the love of my life and I miss him every day. I wish he were still here with me. But he had such an active, brilliant mind. If he had to go, I'm glad it was quick."

She shook her finger at him.

"Why do people do it?" she demanded.

"Do ...?"

"Why do people waste money and energy and resources dragging out a death?"

"Oh, well ..."

"It's just not right!"

Lance looked across McMahon Drive at the brown arroyo stretching east and tried to remember the last time Albuquerque had enjoyed rain. The average rainfall for Albuquerque was just less than ten inches. Over half of that usually fell between July and October. But the weather forecasters regularly commented on the effects of a long term drought. A drought in the desert, isn't that redundant? Shaking his head he turned toward the Vigil's home. His friends, also parishioners, had asked him to come by to sit with them while they put down an aged family pet. Their sheltie provided wonderful companionship over the last decade and a half and now there were too many aches, pains and illnesses. A local veterinarian provided a home visit service. Lance really didn't know what was involved but he had agreed to share the experience with Norm and Cecilia.

Cecilia met him at the door. A short woman who needed a wide passage, she normally displayed a cheerful face but today she looked serious and tense. She ushered Lance into the den where they found Norm watching a man lay out what appeared to be a rubberized sheet on the floor. Norm shook hands with Lance, thanking him for coming. Goldie, the sheltie, lay off to the side. She raised her head when Lance entered the room and then lay back.

Norm introduced Dr. Hernandez to Lance and the vet stood to greet him. He then began to explain to the Vigil's what he intended to do.

"When you are both ready for me to do this, I am going to give her a shot that will sedate her and will also lessen the chance of her vomiting. Then I'll follow up with a shot to stop her heart and lungs. It will be a peaceful process. You may stay in the room with her or go somewhere else in the house and I'll call you back."

Norm pointed at the black sheet on the floor. "That thing protects our carpet from any accidents I guess."

"Well, actually it does more than that. If you notice the edges..." He made a circular motion indicating what he described. "That's a zipper. I'll be able to close her up in a bag and take her to my office. Like I told you before, I'll have her cremains back to you in a couple of days."

Cecilia motioned toward Lance and said, "Reverend Carroll is our pastor. If you don't mind, I'd like for him to say a little prayer for Goldie. I know that probably sounds ..."

Lance interrupted her, "Not at all Cecilia. I'll be glad to."

And he did just that. Lance offered a simple prayer thanking God that the Vigil's had enjoyed such a companionable pet all these years and blessing them because they were caring for Goldie with a loving act. Just before he began the prayer Lance sensed that Hernandez had visibly tensed when Cecilia had identified Lance as a pastor. After the prayer concluded he saw a scowl on the vet's face.

Norm arranged chairs for Lance and the Vigil's to watch the procedure. Both of them rubbed Goldie's back and said kind things to her. In a surprisingly short time the dog died and the vet had her zipped up and out the door into his SUV. Lance told the Vigil's he was glad they wanted him present while they said good-bye to their pet and they, again, thanked him for coming.

Outside Lance walked over to the veterinarian and watched him finish packing things into his car.

"Impressive service you provide."

Hernandez turned toward him. The scowl returned.

"You agree it's a good thing to put down an aging, ill pet?"

"Yes, I do." Lance nodded his head.

"But you preacher types oppose the humane treatment of aged, ill people." He bit off his words sharply.

Lance's mouth was open. Quickly he said, "Preacher types? You assume we all have the same agenda?"

"Don't you?" Hernandez had firmly expressed his opinion. Now he looked away as if he were less sure of himself.

"No, we don't. Any opinion you can find floating around out there will be voiced by some minister or other."

"So, you might consider ..."

"Dr. Hernandez, you have a strong emotional attachment to this issue. Why is that?"

The vet turned to slide the door of his SUV closed and then shrugged his shoulders. Turning back to Lance he said, "It has to do with my mother's long, agonizing death and what a preacher said to me."

"So, you didn't get the kind treatment which you, yourself, give to people like the Vigils."

"If you want to put it that way, yeah."

"I'm sure not all veterinarians agree with the way you dispatch old dogs."

"Most do."

"But there are some complex arguments, aren't there?"

"Not so much."

Lance nodded his head. After a moment he said, "Well, there are pretty complex arguments about end of life decisions for people."

"Right," said Hernandez stomping around the front of his SUV. "And the

bottom line is you can't really help people."
He slammed the door and drove off.

Lance sighed.

"Dad, can I ask you something?"

Lance stood behind his desk chair. He
tossed some papers onto his desk and waved
Gayle into the room.

Gayle sat on an upholstered footstool
that got pushed around the room serving as
chair, table and occasionally a footstool.
Lance settled into his favorite rocking chair.

"What's up?"

"We're trying to help a friend with an
issue."

"We?"

"Well, one of my friends and me. See,
we have another friend who has this
problem."

"Uh-huh."

"What would you think if you found out
I was pregnant?"

"But you're not."

"Of course not. But what if I was?"

Lance frowned, put an elbow on the arm
of the rocking chair, rested his chin in his
hand and tapped his nose with his fore-
finger.

"One of your friends is pregnant." A flat statement.

"Yes sir."

"So this friend is your age? Sixteen? Not more than seventeen."

"Seventeen, I think."

"That would be a bit young to get married. I assume your friend is single."

"Right. And marriage isn't an option. She's not ready for marriage and wouldn't marry him anyway."

"Do you know who she has told?"

"Whom."

Lance's eyes grew large for a moment. "Okay Miss Fixer. You can take time out from resolving your friend's issues to correct your father's grammar."

Gayle squirmed. "Sorry. Didn't mean to side track us."

"Do you know whom she has told?"

"Nobody else."

"Her parents?"

"No."

"The boy?"

"No!"

Lance rocked for a moment.

"So what's your role in this? What are you and your friend doing for her?"

"Listening. Talking. Dad, we don't know what to do or say. She mostly just cries."

"Listening's always a good start. You can be a good friend. But, of course, she'll need more than just friends pretty soon."

Lance leaned forward. "What do you need from me?"

Gayle looked at her father's face. "I just want to know that you know."

"I'm glad you want me to know."

Gayle stood and started to leave the room but turned.

"So why is seventeen too young to get married? How old was Mary when she had Jesus?"

"I don't think anyone really knows."

"But she could have been barely a teenager."

"Could have been. Where'd you hear that?"

"One of your sermons."

"Right. Of course."

"And another thing - how did you know I wasn't the one who is pregnant?"

Lanced chuckled. "Everything would have been different. The words might have been the same, but everything would have been different."

At that moment Frank waddled into the room and sidled up to Lance. When Lance lowered his hand toward the dachshund Frank licked his fingers. Lance laughed and stood up.

"Time to go outside, boy?"

Lance decided to join his friend and they wandered into the backyard.

Frank began his nose-to-the-ground routine, searching for just the right spot to do his business.

"Frank, ol' buddy, you're something else. You have no words yet you communicate very clearly. You are always polite in your requests and you are fastidious with the messes you make. Maybe I should learn something from you."

How many unmarried pregnant teenagers have there been? Lance wasn't sure he wanted to know the answer to that question. In his first pastorate he had been surprised by a couple who wanted advice. He thought they had contacted him to set up a wedding. Oh what a naive, idealistic minister he was. The church, a small Presbyterian congregation on the outskirts of

San Marcos Texas, frequently called new graduates like Lance from Austin seminary. He was sure he had found an ideal first congregation. They were mostly young to middle-aged with children from birth to high schoolers. They seemed to pay attention to every word of his sermons, made gushing compliments, and invited him into their homes. One of those homes happened to introduce him to a recently capped RN who would within a year become Mrs. Carroll.

Lance stood at the door of the church following just his second sermon for his new flock when an attractive couple asked for an appointment. He already knew they were students at Southwest Texas State University. The school's administrative building dominated San Marcos and is visible for miles around the Hill Country town. Southwest Texas had a name change soon into the twenty-first century to Texas State University at San Marcos. It's the only Texas school that can boast a United States president, Lyndon Johnson, as an alumnus.

Well, why does a student couple want an appointment with a minister? They want to get married, right? Sure, that must be it. Lance had already learned that Conrad and Wanda were engaged. Lance recalled the beatific smile stretching his face when Conrad asked him, "How should we go about telling our parents that Wanda's goin' to have an abortion?"

"Actually," Wanda interrupted, "We probably want to wait until afterwards to tell them."

In less than a second Lance's smile morphed from genuine to artificial. "I've only been a pastor for two weeks," Lance remembered wanting to shout at them. What was that? A quarter of a century ago, for his own part not married yet, no children - another life-time.

Mi Casa Memorial Service for Zinnia Foster

Lance prayed, as he said he would, and then invited participation by others. A stout woman in a white dress, obviously a staff uniform, stood up.

"My name is Miranda and I waited on Miss Zinnia when she could come to the cafeteria. Then I took meals to her room. She was a sweetheart wasn't she? Yeah. You would say, 'How are you Miss Zinnia?' and the next thing you know she has you talking about yourself. And she remembered I have two boys and a girl. I mean, the people we serve here are all special and I don't mean any disrespect but Miss Zinnia wasn't always just about herself. How could she do that? I mean, you know, she was dying of cancer. I'll miss her."

Albuquerque Journal
January 13, 2014
Judge: Docs Can Prescribe Meds for Aid
in Dying
by Scott Sandlin

State law provides a fundamental right to a terminally ill, competent patient to choose a physician's aid in getting prescription medications that will allow a peaceful death, a state judge ruled Monday in a seminal case. ...

Chapter Seven

Lance walked to the front door of the church to see who had rung the bell. Jennifer Garcia saw him in the dimly lit hall and waved.

Opening the door he said, "Come in. Get out of the cold."

She danced in quickly allowing him to close the door behind her.

"Not that it's so warm here in the hall."

"Brrr!" She hugged herself. "Why don't you have some heat on?"

"Oh I do, in the office." He gestured down the hall. "In fact I had just climbed up on the secretary's desk to re-aim the vent. Changing from air conditioning to heating we re-route the air flow. The secretary doesn't like cold air on her neck but she wants the warmth."

Lance led Jennifer through the secretary's office into his study.

"Speaking of the secretary ... ?" Jennifer raised her eyebrows with the unfinished question.

Lance pointed at a conference chair and moved behind his desk to his chair.

"Except for me all the church staff is part time. She'll be here sometime after noon. Supposedly she shows up at one o'clock which only means she's sure to be here before two. The janitor is part time meaning he's never here when things break or people want it warmer or cooler or anything needs changing or rearranging."

"Do they have seminary courses in ventilator rearranging?"

"They should. That would be more interesting than Hittite sacrificial practices."

"They have a class in that?"

"Actually I think I skipped that one. But that's not why you dropped by, is it." He wasn't asking a question.

"No," she said and then her face lost any expression. For several moments she simply stared at Lance. "I don't know ... I have no idea what to do."

"What's been said to you?"

"Nothing. I mean no one has officially asked me anything or made an accusation."

"Somebody has told you something."

"Sure. Willow and another nurse took me aside this morning, the moment I returned to the office. They said there were rumors that Zinnia committed suicide and that I helped her."

"What did you think of that?"

"I was appalled. Why would anyone believe I would do something like that? That's against the law. And besides that's not what hospice nurses do. I wouldn't do that."

"Could anyone make a case against you?"

"I don't see how? Zinnia wasn't injected with anything that I know of over the last several weeks. Of course she took a lot of meds by mouth, mostly pain relievers. There might be something there. But the only case against me is I did my job."

"Everybody who knows you knows that."

"I helped make her comfortable during her last days. That was my job. Why would someone turn my job against me?" She stifled a sob.

"I'm sorry you're going through this. And I am pleased that you came by to see me. I was going to find a way to see you."

"See me?"

"Uh-huh. To put it mildly, this is a stressful situation. I'm concerned about how you are handling this."

Jennifer didn't respond. They sat for a moment and then Lance offered to get a cup of coffee for Jennifer. She declined with a smile.

"Do you have a part time waitress who happens not to be here at the moment?"

He laughed. "She's not here now, but then she never is because she doesn't exist.

"Tell me, Jennifer," he continued, "you were horrified - you said 'appalled' - that anyone would accuse you."

"That just makes me cringe."

"As it should. But what about the idea that Zinnia might have wanted to commit suicide? Any thoughts about that?"

Jennifer sat back and looked through the open door into the secretary's office. After thinking about it she turned back to Lance and shrugged.

"You don't know?" he said.

"Hmmm, maybe. I'm not positive one way or the other." She hesitated again and then said, "She loved life but hated her pain."

"Yeah, I saw that."

"One time she told me, 'I know I can't get better and I'm not sure I can stand getting worse.' When I responded we were doing everything possible to relieve her pain she said, 'The one thing you cannot do is remove the pain.' I said, 'I would if I could.'

She said, 'No, you can't and you won't.' I didn't quite understand what she meant so I didn't say anything to that."

"What might she have meant other than it was not humanly possible to eliminate her cancer and the pain it caused?"

"Right. That's the obvious primary meaning I heard in her words. And that's the only thing I considered her to be saying until this minute. It occurs to me in talking with you that she might have meant something else."

Lance raised a hand inviting her to proceed.

"She might have been saying that she knew I could not be the one to assist her with a suicide. She might have been saying that she understood she had no right to invite me in to a conspiracy to remove her pain by precipitating her death."

"If that is what she meant - and we really can't know for sure - but if it was what she meant, she was correct, wasn't she?"

"I don't know what she meant. I only just now thought of this. I don't know. But, yes, if she meant that, then she was dead right. Oh!" Tears burst from her eyes and she flailed her hands about.

"It's just an expression, Jennifer." Lance stood and pushed a tissue box across his desk to where she could reach it.

"That was so dumb!"

"No, it's just a common expression. You didn't mean anything by it."

"But it sounds like I was making a stupid joke."

"I didn't laugh."

"This isn't funny."

"No, you're distressed and not editing your words."

"What am I going to do, Lance?"

"I think we need to find where this rumor is coming from. See if we can stop it at the source."

"There can't be a large number of suspects."

"We need that detective from *Murder She Wrote*."

Zinnia had introduced herself to Lance after Sunday worship. She informed him she wanted to become a member of his church. He led her back into the sanctuary where she sat in the back pew and he placed himself one row in front of her.

"I'd like to come visit your home, maybe bring my wife Willow with me if we can fit it into her schedule. But why don't you give the highlights of your decision to be a part of First Light Presbyterian?"

She told him she was a fairly new widow and had discovered too many memories in the church she had shared with her husband.

"He was such an active part of the church, taught classes, presided over the presbytery, worked with the youth - all wonderful memories for me - but it's too much, too close."

Lance said he understood and he believed FLPC would be delighted to welcome her as a new member.

Lucinda Dominguez never failed to have her hair styled every two weeks. She lived her life punctually in every detail. The fact that the smooth talking weather forecaster promised light sleet this afternoon could not keep her from Alistair's Hot Comb.

Alistair popped the pink cape in front of her and sailed it protectively over her burgundy wool sweater and matching skirt.

"Well now, my dear," he purred, "we have got to hide those roots."

"You always know what's best, Alistair."

He frowned and pushed and pulled at her hair. He tsked, tsked, and even growled. "Oh my poor baby. Someone has mistreated you."

Lucinda turned her head quickly. "What have you heard?"

"Heard? I have heard nothing. But your hair tells me you are deeply stressed."

"You know that? From my hair?"

"Sweetie! I always know your emotions from your hair."

"Oh dear." She sank into the chair.

"What is it, darling? You cannot keep anything from me, you know."

"Well, I know. But I can't tell you what is going on."

Alistair leaned toward her, took her chin in his hand and shook his head. "This is a one chair shop, sweetheart. You're my only concern until four o'clock. Who can you trust if not Alistair?"

He stepped around behind her and began to thumb-pressure massage her shoulders. "Such tension! You're suffering abuse somewhere."

"Oh, that feels so good. I am tense. But no one is abusing anyone. It's just ..."

"Just?"

"Well one of our clients died."

"All of your clients die, sooner or later."

"Of course. That's not unusual. But in her case. You see, I was cleaning out her room, collecting her personal effects and so on and, well, I found an empty pill bottle in the drawer beside her bed." She turned to give Alistair a meaningful look. Whatever reticence she had about discussing her work evaporated in a brief second.

"So?"

"The bottle was nearly empty but the date on the bottle showed it was fairly new."

"What was in the bottle?"

"A rather strong pain reliever."

"So what does that mean?"

"It might mean her death was caused by an overdose."

"Ah, poor dear." Alistair rubbed his chin. "She couldn't take it anymore."

"Well, no. But the thing is - I don't really know - but I just feel that she needed help."

"Help? What kind of help?"

"Oh, you know, someone to parcel out the pills, hand her a glass of water, and encourage her to go through with it."

"Hmmm." The beautician ran his fingers through Lucinda's hair. "Could be, could be. Wasn't there a story like that in Texas. Or was it Alabama?" He took her under an arm and pulled her out of the chair. "Over here, dear heart. We need to start with the shampooing. Sit your sweet self down and lean back." He turned on the sprayer and soaked her hair.

She purred as he massaged her scalp. "That feels so good."

"I know it does. Of course it does."

Lucinda purred some more.

"Did you take the bottle?"

She scowled at him. "Of course not! I left it right where I found it."

"So who has it?"

Lucinda swept her eyes around the floor. "I don't know," she murmured.

Alistair cocked an eyebrow at her as they stared at one another in a mirror.

"Hmmm," he crooned.

He toweled her hair dry and pushed her back to his styling chair.

"Now let's see," he clucked. "You know what would worry me?"

"My bangs are too long?"

"No honey. I don't worry about your hair. Alistair always takes care of your hair.

104

I was thinking about your poor dead old lady."

"Oh, right."

"I would worry about her care taker taking advantage. That's what that Georgia story was about."

"I thought it was Alabama."

"Well, wherever. Some gal was befriending old ladies and getting herself written into their wills or receiving expensive gifts. You know that's what I'd want to check on. Did she get anything out of this untimely death?"

"Oh my, that's terrible."

"Yes, it would be."

"Of course, you can't say it was an untimely death," Lucinda objected. "If she hadn't died that day it would have been the next - or before the week was out."

"Still, you never know."

"That's right. You never know."

The smell of hamburger frying and the promise of green chili drew Willow into the Mexican restaurant. She knew the aroma would have caused Gayle to have walked back out the door but Willow had learned to enjoy tacos and burritos and especially sopapillas. She spotted Dorothy toward the back already snacking on chips and salsa.

"Hey, girlfriend, how ya doing?"

Dorothy smiled at Willow's greeting and waved her to a seat. With formalities given and orders taken - Dorothy wanted a chimachanga and Willow decided on a taco salad - Willow asked Dorothy to catch up on her life.

"Kinda boring, actually. The kids are off to college and that leaves me with an empty house and not that much to do."

"Oh, come on, Dorothy, your church can always find plenty for a minister's wife to do."

"You would think so, wouldn't you, but not so much here. Mylan has the church running like clockwork and we have an active, young congregation. They take care of business."

Their dishes arrived and the women took a few minutes to settle into their lunch.

"I'm really glad we ran into each other the other day, Willow, because I need an outside interest - something not connected to our church."

"And ...?"

"Would you be interested in starting a book group?"

Willow looked away and then back at Dorothy. "A book group. That seems to be the thing to do these days. What kind of books did you have in mind?"

"Printed books with covers. I really haven't thought it through. It just seems like a good idea."

"Yes, it does seem like a good idea. Have you asked anyone else?"

"No," Dorothy looked down at her plate. "This is a fresh brain storm on my part. I've not come up with anything else. But, well, what do you think?"

"Um, I don't know. My first thought is that I don't have time. But, what are you thinking? Maybe once a month?"

"Yeah. Something like that."

Willow noticed Dorothy sighed a few times and wasn't sitting particularly straight. She thought that perhaps agreeing to the book club might be of more value for Dorothy than herself, but that wasn't all bad.

"How about we get together some evening soon when we've both had a chance to think about a book or two we want to read?"

Dorothy smiled. "Really? You'd be willing to do that?"

The strong reaction surprised Willow. It would be good for her friend, and maybe for Willow as well.

Mi Casa Memorial Service for Zinnia Foster

The group remained silent for a while, then a large man dressed in denim walked to the front of the room and turned toward his audience.

"I'm Sid. My name's Sidney but everyone here calls me Sid. I fix things around this place. I knew about Miss Zinnia before she came because, well my granddaughter got pregnant. None of us were very happy about that since she wasn't married. But you know how these kids are. I only had one kid and only the one grandchild so I'm all about spoiling children and giving them all my attention. When she turned up pregnant I wanted to help. Sure that's not what you want for your granddaughter but you still love her. But she kinda disappeared from my life. I couldn't live with that. I thought I would die. I love my girls, my daughter, and granddaughter. But then one day, there she was. I was so happy to see her. Well, I'm sorry; I'm going on too much. But the bottom line was Miss Zinnia had helped her straighten out her life. And the important thing - I'm sorry. Just a minute. I'm sorry. Okay, well, she told me

the most important thing Miss Zinnia helped
her with was the realization that her
Granpop would still love her no matter what.

"Thank you Miss Zinnia, thank you."

Chapter Eight

Nancy pulled on her hoodie and absent-mindedly rubbed her belly. She was almost to the front door of the two-bedroom adobe house where she lived with her parents when her mother called to her.

"Nancy, slow down. You get away so fast in the mornings anymore; we don't have time to talk. I come home so late from work. I never see you."

Nancy's mother worked a later shift as cashier at the Costco in Rio Rancho. Her father also worked late part-time as a security guard at the Central New Mexico Community College West Side Campus. The West Side campus in the west mesa area of Albuquerque was just south of Rio Rancho. Nancy's father had taken a disability semi-retirement as a result of a back injury doing construction work. He had to find a part-time job because his family couldn't live on his benefits and his wife's pay.

"I need to get to school, Mama. Rosita and Gayle are waiting for me."

"Well, give your Mama just one minute, please. I have something for you to think about."

"Okay, sure, what is it."

Nancy's mother was a small woman who had to look up to her daughter who had her father's height.

"Just something to consider."

Nancy became aware, almost as a surprise to her, that her mother looked very tired. She had always been the spark-plug dynamo of the family. Right now, though, her face as well as her body seemed to sag. Maybe, Nancy thought, I've been so wrapped up in my own dark secret, I haven't paid any attention to my mother.

"Things are pretty tight, you know, and not getting any better. It may be - and I just want you to think about this - maybe you should drop out of school after the Christmas break and go to work."

Nancy pulled both hands to her face.

"Maybe for a few months, honey, and then you could go back and catch up with your friends."

"Mama," she said through her fingers.

"I don't know how much longer your father can work. I just don't know ..."

Nancy turned to the door but didn't open it yet.

"It's something to think about. That's all."

Deloit jumped off the bus at the stop on Central Avenue. He had ridden half his lifetime he thought from his home in Rio Rancho south to this stop in Southwest Albuquerque. Now he would wait about thirty minutes - he hoped not more - to catch a bus heading east into the center of the city. These trips never went smoothly. But even with a few bumps he would see his father in about an hour. In fact, the second bus ran on time so, forty minutes later, after a four block hike from where he exited the bus, Deloit was staring at a bright, white building on Roma street. Not too much later his father was ushered from his jail cell into a room where they could talk.

Deloit always began with a recounting of how much money he had made from his jobs and what bills he was able to pay. His father interrupted him after a few minutes with some apparent good news.

"The attorney says they have lowered the bail demands, so maybe I can come back home for a while."

"That sounds great Dad."

"Well, it means I don't have to sit out my time waiting for the trial here in jail. It would be a lot better news if someone would give me my job back."

Deloit let the implications of all of this sink in. His father had been laid off several months earlier. The two of them managed during the summer and early Fall because he had some severance pay. After that stopped and no new employment offered itself they began eating up a savings account the father had set up with the intention of providing a college education for his son. In a rash moment Deloit's father had shoplifted a watch. He was immediately caught and had been in jail now for several weeks.

His mother had died when he was a baby and Deloit had no memory of her. His father never spoke of her. Her absence was not particularly an issue for the two of them. She just didn't exist. The two men were the family and they managed quite well. But then the economy turned sour and the company where his father worked downsized as a first step toward leaving

New Mexico completely. After his father's arrest Deloit realized he had never seen the man deal with a crisis before. He didn't know how his father dealt with the grief of losing his wife. He now began to wonder if maybe his dad had not grieved her loss. Maybe he didn't know how to cope with stress. Obviously Deloit would have to learn some coping skills.

"Do you know how soon you might be able to come home?"

"A few days. No, I don't know exactly."

"Yeah, I hope it's soon." The only thing Deloit could think about was the need to buy more groceries. It was awful to have his father in jail, but at least that way he didn't have to feed him.

With her husband gone Zinnia emerged from her grief with a need to reassess her life. Her first inclination was to travel. She and Mr. Foster had frequently discussed places in the world they wanted to see so she reasoned it might be an appropriate tribute to his life for her to see the world they had wanted to investigate together. Between his shrewd investments and insurance policies she could go as often and as far as she desired. With that in mind she invited Victoria Roybal, Betsy Holmgren and Penny Rainier to collaborate on an African safari. Their sharing of ideas didn't go anything like she planned. It just so happened that Betsy and Penny had invited Victoria into a collaboration they were considering.

Meeting in a nice restaurant on Central Avenue in the Nob Hill area, Betsy kept pushing Zinnia about retiring from teaching. Zinnia insisted she wasn't ready to let go of her "children."

"After all, you know, since Mr. Foster and I never had kids of our own ..."

"Oh we know you love the young people," said Betsy. "I'm just trying to raise a larger question than where you want to go jaunting around this summer."

"I want to see the world. That's the answer to a pretty large question."

At this point the waiter served them their tilapia and they oohed and aahed over the presentation of the plate.

But Penny wasn't ready to eat. "You know, Zinnia, I don't see it, myself."

"Don't see what?"

"I don't see you lusting to venture around the world."

"Well ... I wouldn't say that I lust after Carnival Line cruises."

"No, you don't," agreed Victoria. "What you really want to do is rescue wounded youth."

Zinnia looked at her friends. "Yes, and I do that. That's my job."

"It is," Betsy shook her head, "and it isn't."

"Okay, it's more than my job. I spend time with my students after class and I ..."

"We know," smiled Penny. "We've listened to you describe your passion for working with your students."

"Particularly your girls," added Betsy.

"Which reminds me," said Zinnia, "after we finish here I need to go pick up Cathy, she was in my remedial math class last semester, and ..." Victoria slapped the table and the three friends laughed.

Victoria leaned toward Zinnia and said, "You just don't quit do you?"

"So?"

Penny and Betsy exchanged a look. Victoria tried to conceal a smile. Zinnia leaned back raising her hands.

"How about getting out of the class room and just do the extracurricular contact with the girls?" Betsy's eyebrows practically disappeared into her bangs.

"I don't quite ..."

Penny began poking the table cloth with her knife as though she was charting an argument. "Our husbands left the four of us well positioned so we don't have to work. What if we created a business that provided counseling and tutoring for distressed high school students?"

"A mentoring program," continued Victoria, "Maybe focused on teen pregnancies."

"Do you mean ...?"

"What we mean," said Victoria, "is we want you to be a full-time fixer for your girls."

"Yeah," laughed Betsy. "Do the extracurricular and skip the curricular."

Zinnia never left the state of New Mexico after that night.

Mi Casa Memorial Service for Zinnia Foster

After Sid returned to his seat the group stayed quiet until Lance assumed everyone who meant to speak had done so. Just before he took to his feet Jennifer came forward.

"Hello everyone, I'm Jennifer Garcia. I'm a hospice nurse and I was assigned to Miss Zinnia. Like all the wonderful staff here my job, my purpose is to serve my patient. Our hospice has frequently helped with patients here at Mi Casa and Mrs. Foster was one more, but more than just another patient. Being a hospice nurse is a meaningful ministry. I have always been glad that I chose this career path. But, well, you can guess that it gets heavy, some days even depressing. Dying is a private, personal, internal experience. That's my opinion watching from the sidelines. That means nurses and staff people in a facility like this don't get a lot of thank-yous. I'm not telling you anything you don't already know. And, as I think about it, I don't remember that Miss Zinnia ever said thank you to me. But there was just something in her face, her touch that showed appreciation. I'm glad we have a few minutes here to celebrate her life.

I personally - and maybe you will let me speak for you - I'm glad I knew Miss Zinnia."

Chapter Nine

Yellow leaves rustled through the half-empty parking lot of the public golf course. The overcast sky suggested the autumn day might be too cold for golf but actually the temperature had climbed into the fifties. Lance sat on the back bumper of his SUV in his khaki pants and dark red sweater tying the laces on his shoes.

"You want to go ahead and give me my five dollars now?" A heavy-set middle-aged man approached wearing dark pants and a plaid sweater.

"Mac, when have you ever won any money off me?" Lance sneered.

"Come to think of it, you never paid me for any of those sermon ideas I gave you."

"Like a Catholic priest could come up with a sermon idea."

A third voice interrupted, "Christians at war! Another typical fall afternoon."

Both Lance and Mac laughed at the barb received from their friend and fellow golfer Rabbi Benjamin whom they usually called Benny. Benny, a small, swarthy, older man wore bright blue pants and a dark navy windbreaker.

Mac looked around and then asked, "Leonard late again?"

"So what's new?" said Benny.

"Uh, he called," said Lance. "We're to get the carts and sign in. He'll be here before we tee off."

"Maybe, maybe not," grumbled Mac.

"So what's new? But I already said that," said Benny.

Fortunately by the time the three golfer ministers loaded their clubs on the carts, paid the green fees (Benny paid for Leonard), practiced a few putts, stretched their backs and drove to the first tee, Leonard arrived.

Tall, slender, and older but probably not quite Benny's age, Leonard arrived in plaid pants and a pink cardigan sweater.

"Please," insisted Mac who was about to hit his tee shot, "stand out of my field of vision."

"Good heavens," said Benny, "as late as you are, you certainly had time to dress appropriately."

"What! This is right out of Golf Digest. This is what that young British golfer wears."

"No," said Lance, "Annika Sorenstam is Swedish."

Mac laughed. "Paula Creamer is more like it."

"Sorry I'm late," said Leonard, ignoring the jibes. "Had a parishioner who needed counseling."

Mac picked up his tee and threw his driver into the bag, obviously disgusted with his shot. "Counseling? What sort of counseling does a Unitarian give? You don't repent of anything do you?"

Lance stood from teeing his ball. "Was she offended because you accidently expressed an opinion during Sunday's homily?"

"Leave him alone," said Benny. "He can't help it if he doesn't have the convictions of his courage."

"I was going to feel sorry for beating you three so badly today, but nah. I don't think so now."

"Oh man," said Mac, "the ugly things we say to one another. No wonder Lance calls us the 'Unholy Handicappers'."

Lance and Benny rode together in the first cart because they both typically sliced their drives or pushed shots to the right. In the second cart Mac and Leonard joined to look for their balls on the left side of the fairway where they both pulled or hooked their shots. True to form they headed in opposite directions. Mac was the only one to find his tee shot. By the time they finished the first nine holes the foursome had collectively lost twelve balls. Not bad by their usual standards. They stopped in the clubhouse to buy new drinks but more to the point, to find the restroom and relieve themselves of what they drank over the last two hours. Two other sets of golfers took advantage of the Unholy Handicappers' delay and rushed to the tenth tee. When the four ministers carted back to the course they discovered they would have to wait a spell before they could continue their game.

Mac and Benny sat in their respective carts. Leonard swung his driver mumbling about the keys to hitting a fade. Lance leaned against his cart chuckling about some sly dig Benny offered critical of Leonard's golfing style.

"What was that Rabbi?" grunted Leonard.

"You don't want to know," Lance answered. "But hey, we've got a few more minutes. I've got a serious question for you guys."

"We don't do serious on Wednesdays," said Mac.

Benny squinted against the sun. "We could do serious for a few minutes."

Mac nodded. "Sure, we could."

"You know what we could do while waiting," said Leonard, "we could sing. I bet we could make a pretty good quartet. Let's try 'My Wild Irish Rose.' "

Mac swatted Leonard's shoulder. "You can't make a quartet with three basses and a monotone."

Leonard rubbed his shoulder. "I sing tenor."

Benny threw a questioning look Mac's way. "I'd sing lead. Who's the monotone?"

Mac laughed. "I am. Can't sing a lick."

Benny shrugged, "Makes you a baritone and I imagine Lance can sing bass."

Mac indicated Leonard with his thumb. "Song-meister here interrupted what Lance was saying."

Lance turned toward the two carts as if closing off their discussion from outsiders. "What if a parishioner asked you, in a confidential moment, about helping a friend whose condition is seriously terminal, uh, helping that friend ease into the hereafter?"

Leonard removed his cap and rubbed his head. "I believe the man meant serious."

"Assisted suicide," said Mac.

"Right," Lance affirmed.

"Serious problem," Mac continued. "Catholic dogma doesn't allow it."

Benny nodded his head. "Most Jews agree. You can't do that. Although Reformed Jews like me are more open to the possibility. But you're probably talking about breaking the law. No matter where you come down on this as a moral issue, you can't encourage breaking the law."

Leonard nodded, "You guys have told me many times that Unitarians don't have a moral code but we go along pretty well with what Benny just said: don't treat the law casually. However ..."

"However, what?"

"Well, I think New Mexico's law is vague on this point."

"I doubt that," huffed Mac.

"No, really. This is an issue in the courts."

"In the courts! How?" asked Benny.

"Well," said Leonard, "I don't remember."

"That's helpful," groused Lance.

"I know it's important. I heard a doctor explaining the legal issues."

Mac laughed. "Are you sure it wasn't a lawyer explaining medical issues?"

Leonard pointed at Mac. "In this case, it could have been."

Mac touched Lance's arm. "Are we helping? Is this even close?"

"Yeah. More or less."

A golfer waiting behind the four debaters broke into their discussion, "You guys gonna play this hole, or what?"

Mac waved at Lance, "Your honors."

Lance shook his head. "Leonard's in the tee box. Ready man hits. That's the way we play."

Benny and Lance watched the other two hook their tee shots, one worse than the other.

"This is a real question, isn't it," Benny observed.

"Oh yes, it's real."

Benny drove his ball dead right into some trees. Lance teed his ball and tried to concentrate on hitting to the middle of the fairway. He successfully drove his ball further down course than the other three and further off the fairway as well.

In the cart Benny asked how quickly the decision has to be made.

"It's a done deal. It already happened."

Benny whistled.

They found Benny's ball up against a tree so he claimed an unplayable lie and threw the ball into the fairway.

"I'll have to take a stroke for that," he said.

"At least one."

"One's enough. I'll triple bogey this hole anyway."

They carted up to where they expected to find Lance's ball - no problem, it was in plain sight - in the next fairway. While waiting for Mac and Leonard to play and then for a foursome in the adjoining fairway where Lance's ball rested to pass them, Benny took up the question again.

"Back there Mac said something about 'assisted suicide.' Is that what you're talking about?"

When Lance didn't respond, Benny went on. "You know there's a difference between that and aiding one's death."

"Oh, really. What's the difference?"

"No idea. I think that's an issue for lawyers and judges. Doesn't much matter to terminal patients.

"Is your church member facing arrest or a legal entanglement?"

"Man, I really ..." Lance yanked off his cap and ruffled his hair. "I really meant to keep this a hypothetical case. But no, no cops yet. It's a matter of gossip. And if the gossip isn't controlled, somebody may come snooping around. An investigation ..." Lance grabbed a club and swatted his ball without aiming at anything. The ball fired into a tree and bounced back rifling between the two men.

"You're getting upset, Lance. Let's just walk it back to our fairway. You can share my triple."

Neither golfer said another word until they stood at the next tee waiting for Mac and Leonard to tee off and then each one elected to hit mulligans.

"A distraction is what you need," said Benny.

"What do you mean?"

"Well, gossip is only hot and heavy about you until your neighbor makes a bigger fool of himself. Then your neighbor is the topic until you become stupid enough to replace him again."

"So, I need a distraction."

"Right. There must be some way you can change the focus of attention."

Lance stepped forward and threw his ball on the ground. As he began to wind up for a powerful swing Benny hissed, "Get your head back into golf before you kill someone with an errant shot."

"Where's his head been?" asked Leonard.

"Hey," yelled Mac. "You two been breaking the rules? No talking shop on the course!"

Lance began to laugh. He picked up his ball, walked back to the cart to change clubs and laughed some more. Walking back to the tee box he teed his ball properly giggling all the way. After driving the ball straight down the fairway, he turned and laughed at Mac again.

"What on earth is so funny," asked Mac.

"Benny has been advising me on rumor mongering. The way to quell one rumor is to start another."

"That's not funny," said Leonard.

"No. Of course not," agreed Lance. "But I just came up with the perfect rumor.

"Uh-oh," muttered Benny.

"I don't think I want to hear this," said Mac.

"It probably involves a Catholic priest and a nun," said Leonard.

"Or a nunnery," Benny answered.

Lance just dropped into the golf cart giggling.

"Don't be in a hurry to leave. I have one more item to discuss." Amanda Griegos waved her hands motioning the nurses to stay seated. "Dr. Melvin," she addressed the young man seated to her right. "You've done your part. You don't need to stay for this." Pleased by that word, the doctor quickly fled the room. Ms. Griegos, a lead nurse for the hospice presided over regular weekly meetings to review the patients under their care. The nurses who served those patients met with a physician to plan therapies and evaluate the treatment of terminal patients whose prognosis expected them to exit this life sometime less than half a year away.

"We've suffered a lot of negative vibrations about Zinnia Foster's death and I want to make a few positive affirmations to see if we can't boost the morale around here." Her comment elicited silence - and then a nervous laugh.

Willow Carroll's brusque voice broke the silence. "What's positive about Zinnia's death?"

"Well, nothing. There's nothing positive about that dear woman's death, Willow. But there are some positives I need to say about you folks."

Chairs squeaked as the nurses sat straighter. This was something they wanted to hear.

"Jennifer stars as one of our stand-out nurses. All of you do excellent work." Amanda deliberately made eye contact with everyone around the table. Besides Willow and Jennifer there were eight other women and one male nurse before Ms. Griegos. "I have to admit I've been, umm, anxious about what I've been hearing concerning her death. But never for one minute have I believed any of you were capable of violating hospice rules, sound patient care, or New Mexico laws. I apologize for not saying that sooner. We've spent a lot of time emphasizing we must all follow the letter of the law and make sure not to give anyone reason to doubt us. Well, that's business as usual for you. And I want you to know that I know that." She offered them an overly exaggerated smile. "Any questions or comments?"

The nurses adopted the posture of schoolchildren hoping no one would speak so they could escape the classroom.

As one might expect, the youngest nurse present spoke up. "You know, this will probably turn out to be one of those best and worst things. You know, like when the one thing you do is both the best thing you could do and the worst thing you could do at the same time."

Since her comment produced only nervous squirming, she attempted to explain. "Well, like if she gave Zinnia some pills to put her out of her misery, that could be a good thing, you know. But if she did this without talking to anybody, like a big secret - I dunno. That could be bad."

An older nurse sitting next to her patted her shoulder. "Kathy, don't make any speeches about this."

Together the nurses gathered their things and left the room.

Albuquerque Journal
January 14, 2014
NM Judge: Patients Have Right to Get
Help in Dying
by Scott Sandlin

... The practice of aid in dying
recognizes that the patient is dying from his
or her underlying disease and allows the
patient to have medication, usually
sedatives, that may be taken at a time of the
patient's choosing to achieve a peaceful
death. Patients who most often choose the
option are those dying of cancer. ...

Chapter Ten

Lucinda Dominguez thanked the floral deliveryman, thus dismissing him and then, since the lobby was vacant at the moment, set about delivering the pot of mums to a room toward the back of Mi Casa's commodious building. The older lady who was the recipient of the flowers slept in a recliner. The blinds were closed shutting off the room from the bright morning sunshine. Lucinda reflexively sniffed the room. The facility director had trained every staff member to be sensitive to odors anywhere in the building. Primarily they were alert to the smells of urine or feces. Any smell at all, even simple stuffiness, which might make someone think "Old Folks Home" required the immediate attention of cleaning personnel. Typical of the tastes of the older clients this room felt overly warm to Lucinda but there were no untoward odors. She quietly left the potted plant on the dresser and slipped out of the room.

On the way back to her receptionist's desk in the lobby she passed the director's office. Finding the door open she stepped inside. "Hallo, Sally," she announced herself.

Sally Ingersoll, a compact woman in her mid-fifties with dark hair and complexion, wearing a stylish green and grey suit, smiled at Lucinda and waved her in.

"What's up, Lucinda?"

"Notice anything?" Lucinda raised both palms and waited.

"Of course. You've had your hair done. That's a very becoming color, muted but elegant."

"Oh, thank you. I think it's the best he's done."

"Well, it really suits you. That is so nice. How are things going up front?"

"Quite well. The new plants at the front door set such a nice scene when people come in."

"I knew you would like them."

"Sally, I was wondering ..."

Sally leaned back in her executive chair. "Yes?"

"About how often do we lose a client?"

Sally tapped a finger on the desk. "Hmmm. We average about a couple of deaths a month. But that figure in itself is meaningless because our people tend to die in twos or threes. We'll go weeks without losing anyone and then, well, you know."

"Yes, I guess I do."

Sally raised an eyebrow. "Why do you ask?"

"Ah, just curious."

"Losing Mrs. Foster spur some thoughts?"

"Uh-huh."

"Funny, isn't it - well, maybe interesting would be a better choice of words. But it is interesting that we can provide a space for an old man or woman who will decline and die and we hardly know they were here and then he'll be gone. We were just doing our job. It's not that we are uncaring; we just didn't learn to know him. And someone like Zinnia moves into our facility and also into hearts. When she dies we hurt. Again, it's our job to see these people through to the death. But that doesn't mean we can't grieve for them."

Lucinda stepped forward and fished a tissue from the box on Sally's desk.

"That's so true, so true," she said and dabbed her eyes.

She waved the tissue in the air as if to pull a thought out of the atmosphere. "What do they call it when old people die in a nursing facility? Old age? Natural causes?"

"Yes, something like that. About eighty percent of the time. Then there's the occasional heart attack. Usually our clients just run out of time."

"Hmmm. Well, I need to get back up front."

"The hair looks wonderful."

As the noon hour approached Sally and her secretary breezed past Lucinda's desk. "We've got that lunch meeting, remember? Be back before two."

Lucinda watched them until they disappeared around the corner of the building. She picked up a couple of sheets of paper from her desk and walked back to the director's office. Against one wall in the outer secretary's office stood several wooden file cabinets. As was often the case in her job she needed to file some papers and so opened a file drawer. She placed the papers she had brought with her on top of the file cabinet and began to rummage through the files in the drawer searching for the right one. Before deciding on the appropriate folder she stepped to the door and looked right and left in the hall. She smiled at the emptiness she saw. Returning to the cabinets she found a different drawer labeled 'Death Certificates.' The folders in this drawer were marked with the year of the deaths. They were arranged in reverse order so the current year's folder was in the front of the drawer. There appeared to be about fifteen or twenty death certificates filed so far for the year. Lucinda quickly looked through them, frowning as she read. A cursory reading showed four different physicians had signed the various documents. Although the cause of death was consistently stated in terse language, she didn't learn much. She replaced those certificates and pulled out the ones for the previous year. A quick count showed thirty deaths in that year. Again she read through them. Six different names appeared at the bottom of the certificates.

"Hmmmpf!" she muttered as she closed the drawer. "Waste of time. Old people just die. That's informative." She also realized that determining who might have been present at the death of each client would require reading each patient chart. And even that wouldn't tell much. She shoved the other file drawer closed and snatched the papers off the cabinet, forgetting her ruse of filing documents.

Walking back to her desk Lucinda heard footsteps behind her and turned as a man passed her on his way out. He smiled and said, "Hello, Miss Dominguez."

She recognized Mr. Reaves, the son of one of Mi Casa's older residents.

"How's your mother," she asked.

Reaves slowed his pace to match that of Lucinda.

"She's doing quite well, thank you. She seemed a bit sad because you lost one of your people. She really liked, uh." He apparently searched for a name.

"Mrs. Foster," Lucinda helped him.

"Yes, right, Mrs. Foster. Nice lady I gather."

Lucinda stopped at her desk.

"Oh yes. Mrs. Foster was a pleasant lady. She'll be missed."

Mr. Reaves waved a goodbye and turned toward the door. Just at that moment Lucinda remembered that he was a detective, or at least some kind of police officer with the Albuquerque Police Department.

She let out a half-giggle, snort.

Reaves turned back to look at her. He raised an eyebrow.

"I just thought ..."

"Yes."

"Well. I wondered if you were here for another reason than just to visit your mother."

"What would that be?"

"Ah, well, do you ever investigate when people die in nursing homes or anything like, you know, or hospitals, or ..." She waved her hands.

"No. Most people die because their time is up. Unfortunately that time comes for all of us." He smiled. "No reason to go nosing around just because someone's number is up. We haven't the time or resources for that."

"Of course."

"Unless you're telling me there was something suspicious going on?"

Lucinda's face turned white.

Detective Reaves burst out laughing. "Don't be upset. I'm not making any accusations."

"Oh, I, well," she spluttered.

He laughed some more as he turned and left her with an acute case of embarrassment.

"The Widows" began their mentoring business and located a small house off of Unser Boulevard for their base of operations. Penny became the business manager/bookkeeper. Betsy wrote a grant and saw to the legal details. Victoria solicited funds from friends (although the women put up most of the financing themselves). And Zinnia provided the talent. She did recruit a couple of school counselors and a variety of mothers to volunteer their service but for the most part Zinnia was the program. She worked harder and put in more hours than she ever had as an "official" class room teacher. And she loved it. She saw her role as a mid-wife/facilitator helping girls manage their education while facing the reality of a surprise pregnancy. Each of the women felt this was why they had come to Albuquerque.

A chief motivator for the women was their clear understanding of New Mexico's teen pregnancy statistics. The national statistics are bad enough. Nearly half of sexually active high schoolers don't use condoms. And authorities believe adolescents account for half of the new sexually transmitted diseases every year. The women were not surprised when Zinnia told them New Mexico consistently ranks in the top three states nationally in unmarried pregnant teens.

From the start Victoria had established the business as a 501-C3 non-profit but one day Penny came to the Booster House, as they called it, to tell Zinnia the "bad" news that they were actually making a profit. She had a speech in mind in which she would explain that they could solve their "problem" in a variety of ways. Zinnia could more carefully keep track of legitimate expenses, something she was reluctant to do. Zinnia felt that everything any of the women did was part of their contribution and there was no need to declare any of that an expense. But Penny was sure she could make the Director understand the need to remain a non-profit. They could also take the profit - whatever it was - and give it away. There were plenty of benevolent enterprises around that would welcome the donation. She entered the front room, furnished as a sitting room with comfortable sofas and chairs, draped walls, all done in pastels and surprisingly empty.

"Yoo-hoo, anybody home?"

A teen who looked to be entering her second trimester rushed around the hall door pointing down the hall.

"I think Miss Zinnia's sick," she said.

Penny found her in her office perspiring and nauseous.

The cancer had hidden, not presenting any symptoms until it had perversely grown to an advanced level in her pancreas.

Victoria called Penny and Betsy and between the three of them Zinnia received the full attention of Dr. Rosario, probably the best oncologist New Mexico could offer. A first-year hospital orderly would have sufficed for all the good medical care could do. Zinnia's cancer, aggressive and malicious, counted down her remaining days.

"What do you think is the best film produced in New Mexico?" Gayle felt her question would enliven the dinner table mood.

Zach had an immediate response. "That Lone Ranger movie with Johnny Depp as Tonto."

"No way," said Gayle. "He looked stupid in that bird's nest headdress and besides he's not even Indian."

"What about the John Travolta movie where those lawyers rode motorcycles to Madrid?" offered Willow.

"I liked 'Fifty to One'," said Lance. "But really 'Breaking Bad' put Albuquerque out front ..."

"As a meth center," interrupted Willow.

"Well, right. I didn't like that too much."

Frank pawed Gayle's leg and she lifted him into her lap.

Willow frowned and said, "Not while we're eating."

"Actually, I'm through."

"You know, I really like 'Longmire' - the Wyoming sheriff," said Zach.

"Oh yeah, the Wyoming sheriff with his law office in Las Vegas, New Mexico," giggled Gayle.

Lance waved his fork. "The whole thing's filmed in New Mexico."

"They're just flat lying to your face," muttered Zach.

Gayle pointed at her brother. "You misspelled 'lying.' "

"What! I'm talking not writing. You can't misspell when you 're talking."

"You can."

"How would you know?"

"I know. I can read your mind, your heart, and your stomach. Actually your stomach does most of your thinking."

"Now you're the one who's lying to me."

"Zach," Willow intruded on the sibling debate, "She's putting you on. That's not lying."

"And it would really be scary if she - or if anyone - could really do that," Lance noted.

"There was a New Mexico production that dealt with deception," said Willow. "Know which one?"

The other three family members shook their heads.

"In Plain Sight."

"Oh yeah," said Gayle, "the one about people brought to New Mexico and put in witness protection."

"Hmmm," said Lance, "hide in plain sight. Tell the truth except for just enough to camouflage the truth."

Chapter Eleven

Lance returned to Mi Casa this time to visit church members living there. Brent and Phyllis Novak were elderly and in poor health. They had no family to care for them and little money to live on, but fortunately had purchased for themselves an excellent long care assisted living insurance policy. The insurance allowed them to move into a small apartment in Mi Casa where they had a bedroom, sitting room and a postage stamp of a kitchenette.

The door was slightly open. Lance knocked and called a hello, which received a quick answer from Brent inviting him in. The old man, carrying maybe a hundred forty pounds on a two-twenty frame, sat in a rocking chair facing the television. A soccer game was in progress. Brent waved at a two-seater divan and Lance sat.

"Who's playing?"

"Foreigners. Brits and Italians."

"Who's winning?"

"Nobody. They rarely score in these games."

"You follow soccer? Ever watch world cup games?"

"I just watch whatever's on. Soccer has two things going for it: lots of green grass and the clock never stops, so there are almost no commercials."

Lance laughed. "Where's Phyllis?"

"Playing bridge."

"Good, glad to hear that. She wasn't feeling well the last time I was here."

"She's not any better. She hasn't felt well in ten years. Neither have I, for that matter. We survive."

"Anything I can do to help?"

"You come and say 'Hey' regularly. That's plenty. By the way you did a good job with Zinnia's memorial."

"Well I was glad there was an opportunity to do that for the staff and residents. I don't think they do many memorial services here but in Zinnia's case it seemed appropriate."

"Yeah. Like I said, we thought you handled it well."

"We'll see how the next one goes. Zinnia's partners in her mentoring business want a service where Zinnia's Girls can say something about her."

"She had a mentoring business? I thought she was a school teacher."

"She had been. But she retired from that and collaborated with friends to help pregnant teens who might have to drop out of school or needed help with some tough decisions."

"So when you say Zinnia's girls, you mean ..."

"The young women who were the clients of her business."

"Uh-huh. No children of her own?"

"Right. But she took on everybody's kids as hers."

Lance looked around as if expecting to see something different, something changed in the room. An old wedding picture of the Novaks adorned one wall. There was no other decoration in the room.

"Anybody say anything about Zinnia's death?" asked Lance.

"Like what? Nobody's said a thing. Even though some other residents knew Zinnia, what would anybody say?"

"Dumb question."

"Maybe not so dumb. You're a smart man. You don't ask questions without a purpose."

"Sometimes."

"No, the staff never says anything. Not anything I've ever heard. They probably think we are hypersensitive about dying ourselves so the topic is verboten."

"I can understand that."

"How are you doing, pastor? You and Willow and the kids getting along all right?"

"Oh we're fine. We're all doing quite well. Better than we were doing this summer."

"What happened this summer?"

"Willow and I repapered a bathroom. Let me tell you! That will stress a marriage. If you can work together repapering a bathroom, that's the grand test of a strong marriage."

Brent barked a laugh and began shaking his head. "No, no, no. The test of a marriage? I don't think so. Let me tell you the tests - I said tests - of a marriage. Have your son, your only child, the joy of your life excel in school and sports and then ship half way around the world and die in a stupid war. Lose your savings in a business that flounders because of a change in tax laws. Downsize your home for all the right reasons but lose your equity and more when your four bedroom home in the best neighborhood won't sell. Abandon golf, tennis and hiking because your pocketbook and your knees can't do it anymore. Try to remember what sex was like but it's been so long you're not sure." Brent paused to stave off a cough and then continued. "Attempt a conversation but it fails because neither one of you can remember what you were talking about. In other words, pastor, strip a relationship down to just the two of you, no diversions, no add-ons, just two people with mixed memories. I believe I can trump your wall-paper story."

Lance remembered a recent visit when he surveyed the front of the University of New Mexico Hospital wondering at the enormity of the building. "If impressiveness could provide cures, Zinnia should do well here," he thought. Inside he received directions to her room and rushed to the elevator. Standing before her room he hesitated before entering. Victoria Roybal had called to tell him Zinnia had been diagnosed with a "bad case of cancer." He had just seen her at church, what was it, about ten days ago? How bad was "bad?"

Inside the room a nurse was fussing with her patient. Zinnia looked pale and drawn. Lance didn't like any part of this. He touched her shoulder. "How are you, Zinnia?"

She turned her eyes toward him; haltingly she raised a hand to his. She licked her lips and almost smiled. "Not so good I'm afraid."

He tried to say something encouraging and fumbled around a bit. Then, because the nurse's demeanor suggested he was intruding, he left.

After Lance left the Novak's apartment he made his way to the facility office. There he found a secretary who smiled and asked how she could help him.

"Ms. Ingersoll, is she in?"

"No, she's gone to Santa Fe. A group of nursing home administrators are meeting with some official at the capitol. It seems we have too much regulation or not enough."

"One or the other."

"Yes. I think it depends on even or odd years."

"So this group goes to Santa Fe a lot?" Lance leaned against the open door frame.

"Not a lot, but quite regularly." She closed a folder on something she had been reading, and then she leaned back in her chair. "We feel like we have one of the best nursing homes in the state and we work hard to keep it that way. But," she grimaced, "we would rather government types didn't pay too much attention to us."

"Because?" Lance encouraged her to continue her train of thought.

"Of course there should be some supervision. Any facility caring for the public should be licensed and regulated to some extent."

"Sure," Lance said.

"But people who poke around looking for problems where there aren't any problems, well they just get in the way of those of us who are doing a good job."

"I'm sure Ms. Ingersoll would say the same if she were here."

The secretary laughed. "Oh I'm afraid I've been quoting her. I don't suppose I've ever had an original thought myself."

"Surely that's not true."

As Lance neared the receptionist desk Lucinda looked up and pointed at him.

"You're Miss Zinnia's pastor, aren't you?"

"Yes, I am."

"Reverend Carroll," she nodded as if to agree with herself that she had gotten it right.

"Yes. Right again."

She pushed back her chair and stood. "I was wondering, that is, what did you think about her death?"

"I thought we lost a wonderful person in Zinnia Foster."

"Uh-huh. But did you think there was anything odd about it?"

"Odd? Well, of course it was too soon. She did marvelous work with young women and we could have benefitted from her gifts for years. But it was really a blessing that she found release from her cancer. Odd? No I wouldn't call it odd."

"Right. Of course you are right in everything you said. But maybe something ..." Lucinda flushed and seemed to think better about what she was about to say.

Lance touched her arm. "You don't like to lose one of your people, do you?"

She sat and pulled a tissue from the box on her desk. She nodded an affirmation.

Chapter Twelve

Lance had dressed in denims to work in the garden and was pulling on his work shoes when Gayle came into the kitchen and told him she needed some clarification.

"Clarification? About what?"

"Well it pretty well boils down to abortion or adoption doesn't it?"

"Ah, your friend's problem." He waved at a breakfast table chair and finished lacing his shoes while she sat down.

"Yeah, we're not very excited about either of those choices."

"Well, the best choice is to not get pregnant in the first place."

Together they said, "A little late for that."

"She just can't get an abortion, can she Dad? That's just wrong."

Lance looked at his daughter and slowly nodded. "It's not good. I'll have to agree with that. But it isn't necessarily wrong in the sense of the worst bad thing anyone can do."

"No, but Dad, it's murder, isn't it?"

"That's a position many of your friends would hold. I don't believe that."

"I've never heard you preach a sermon about it."

"Well I have, indirectly. That's not something you'd pick up on until just recently when your friend turned up pregnant."

"What'd you say?"

"Oh, something along the lines of what Reinhold Niebuhr taught about ..."

"Who's he?"

"Just one of your father's heroes." Willow passed through the kitchen on the way to the garage. She had just caught Lance's last comment.

"A hero?" Gayle straightened in her chair.

"Ah, yes," said Lance. "A preacher, teacher, writer. He had a lot to say about choosing the lesser of evils. Sometimes we get ourselves into a mess where there are no good choices, only not good, bad, and worse ones."

"Well, I'm going to list abortion as bad or worse."

"Okay, what do you and your friends think about adoption. I'd call that a fairly good possibility."

"Giving away your baby?"

Lance raised both arms. "You don't like that one either."

"Well, sure, it's better than abortion, but, no, we don't like that one. Okay, so *I* don't like that one. Not sure about anyone else."

"So what am I s'posed to be clarifying here? You seem to be quite clear in your convictions."

"What I said at first, aren't those the only options."

"No, of course not." Lance counted on his fingers. "First, get married and provide the baby a family."

"Not an option."

"You're pretty sure that wouldn't work?"

"No question about it."

"Okay then, second, abortion."

"No way."

"Third, adoption. Give a childless couple a chance at a family."

"Don't really like it." She waved her hand as if wanting to change the answer. "I mean, that's a great thing for a couple to do, rescue a baby, start their family, whatever. But not a good choice here."

"Okay, that leaves keep the baby and become a single mother."

"Yeah, that has its problems too."

"Uh-huh. That usually means the grandparents get roped into sharing parenting duties. The single mom will have to drop out of school and get a job. It's a hard life."

"I think I'm beginning to get the idea of 'lesser of evils'."

Lance stood. "Help me with some yard work."

Gayle shook her head and jumped up. "Most evil choice. I have good to do. Places to go. People to see."

She turned to leave, hesitated, and then turned back to her father.

"It's really hard isn't it?"

"Uhm, what? What's really hard?"

She leaned back against the doorframe and rubbed her chin. At that moment Lance could see himself in his daughter.

"Keeping a secret. Knowing something that you just can't tell anyone because it could hurt someone. It kind of sits on your heart and presses outward like it wants to escape, but you have to keep it in, and it weighs on you and you don't know if you can continue to hide it."

The tears poured from Lance's normally cheerful girl. He stood and pulled her into his arms.

"You're the best sort of friend. You can carry the weight."

She pushed back and looked up at him.

"I'm sorry, Daddy."

He wiped her cheeks with a shirtsleeve then he smiled at her and proclaimed, "Go and sin no more."

"I haven't sinned all day."

Lance pulled her head toward him and kissed her forehead.

"Maybe so."

She slipped out of the room as Lance nodded his head and whispered, "Very hard."

Zinnia, dressed in a loose housedress, surveyed her room. She had been moved into Mi Casa Senior Care after spending a month at home.

"All right," she said to Lance, "it's better than going back to a hospital bed."

"Yeah," he nodded, "I'd say so."

"But not by much."

He watched as she sat in a rocking chair, one of only two places to sit other than the bed. After she sat down he took the remaining chair.

"What did the doctor tell you about moving here?"

"The monster is out to get me."

"Oh. The doctor said that?"

"Same as." Her head dropped and she shook it. "I guess it's progressing pretty fast. I'm here because I need constant attention."

"Twenty-four hour?"

"No, but close to it."

"How are you feeling?"

"It's really a damn shame!" She ignored his question.

Lance looked surprised. "You're angry aren't you?"

"Hell yes I'm angry. I've got too much to do. I haven't got time to just lie here and die."

"I'm sorry, Zinnia. I'm very sorry."

"No. I'm the one to be sorry. I shouldn't be yelling at you."

"Oh, that's quite all right. In fact, if you'd like, the two of us could yell at God for a while."

She nodded. "You preached a sermon about that once, 'Ten reasons to yell at God.' "

He chuckled. "You remember that?"

"I hadn't. But you reminded me of it just now." After a moment she picked up the thought again. "I may just do that, pastor. But I think I'll do the yelling by myself."

"Okay. But call me anytime."

♥ ♥ ♥ ♥

Lance finished deadheading the rose bushes in his backyard when he scowled at the flower bed. Bending over he pulled a fresh shoot out the ground. As he looked around him he noticed several more of these shoots both in the flowerbed and the yard. At that point he heard a noise in the neighbor's yard so he stepped over to the 'gossip break' in the fence. The Carrolls and their neighbors had agreed the tall cedar fence separating their yards was too restrictive so they cut a break in the top of the fence about halfway along so that for a couple of feet the fence was only four feet tall.

"Hey Clem, got a question for you," he yelled to his neighbor.

Clem, a portly older sanitation engineer (what a successful plumber calls himself) meandered to the fence. "Need a washer replaced?"

"Nothing that complicated."

"That's good. I wouldn't want to have to call my associate."

"Know what this is?" Lance shoved the freshly uprooted plant across the fence.

Clem sniffed once. "Smell that?"

"Yeah, I do. Every time I pull up one of these shoots."

"One of your fledgling stink trees."

"Right. That thing is sprouting all over the place. Stink tree?"

Clem nodded. "Well, they're the children of that tree you have in the corner of your garden. Don't know what its official name is. I've always called them stink trees. If you don't keep after them, you'll have a full forest in your backyard before you know it."

"I think I ought to have the thing cut down."

"Well, might be a good idea. You'll lose some shade if you do."

Lance turned and surveyed his backyard. "I'll lose a lot of trash. That tree drops leaves and seed pods all over the yard."

"Fine with me. I'd be glad to help cut it down but I'd recommend a buddy who's a professional. If you and I do it, one of us will drop a limb on the other. Of course if I'm the dropper and you're the droppee - but it might not work that way. And truthfully I wouldn't want either one of us to get hurt."

Lance laughed and asked Clem to give him his friend's number.

Who is helping and who gets hurt? The young man who introduced himself as Conrad Johansson stood a couple of inches taller than Lance. Blond, blue-eyed, he probably could have come from Gruene or New Braunfels or some other part of German Texas. His girlfriend, Wanda Braun, also a blond but green-eyed, would make a beautiful bride - someday. Lance ushered them into the church's kitchen and sat them at a worktable because, as he explained, the pastor's office in his first ministerial charge wasn't large enough for him to lean back in his chair, much less counsel anyone.

"How can I help you," he smiled, knowing full well that two weeks into this new ministry he would be doing marriage counseling and calendaring a wedding date.

The young man looked at the tabletop and then past Lance to the cabinets behind him. "Pastor Lance," he swallowed, "we've got ourselves into a bit of a fix."

"Oh?"

"Yes, you see, Wanda is, uh, as my mom would say, is in a family way."

"A family way?" Lance was stunned and later was sure it must have shown on his face.

"Right. She's pregnant. It came as something of a surprise."

At the moment Lance doubted if anyone could have been more surprised than he was.

"Oh we know all about birth control," said Wanda. "It's just we were sure we had timed this just right."

"Timed it right?" Lance was dog paddling, quite positive he was about to drown.

"You know," she said, "paying attention to my body's rhythms."

"Uh-huh."

Conrad took up the narrative again. "So, we'd like any advice you can give us about our families."

"Advice? About families?"

"Exactly. We don't really want to tell anyone about this. But, on the other hand, we come from loving parents who've never had a secret in their lives. So what's the best action here? Do we tell them or not?"

"And what do we tell them," added Wanda. "And when?"

"You mean, like, uh, before you start to show or ..."

"Oh she won't show."

"No. We've already made plans for an abortion."

"Huh?" Now Lance was sure he was drowning.

"Yeah," said Conrad. "That's not really the hard part for us."

"An abortion in San Marcos?"

"Oh no. For one thing we wouldn't want to take a chance someone from the school could find out. No, we realize a baby right now is just not the right move for our relationship. We're not ready for marriage - though understand Pastor Lance, we are committed to one another and want a family someday. We just know this would not be good for our education or our careers."

"That couldn't be, uh, inexpensive." Lance frantically tried to create a list in his mind of issues to be discussed.

"Well, no," said the young man, "but finances are not a problem."

The couple spent about an hour with Lance during which time he never successfully finished an intelligent sentence. Remembering this first encounter with a pregnant teenager all Lance could do was shake his head. He had not helped them in any discernable way. Usually in reflecting on it, he felt they had manipulated him to condone their selfish behavior.

Albuquerque Journal
March 13, 2014
Attorney General Appeals Ruling on
Assisted Suicide
by Jon Swedien
... "We feel, win or lose, we need some
decision by the (state) Supreme Court, or at
least the appeals court, that will apply across
the state," ...

Chapter Thirteen

The large room toward the back of the First Light Presbyterian Church building - deemed the fellowship hall by the members - rattled and hummed with the noise of a wedding reception. One of the favorite girls of the church family had grown into a beautiful young lady who one day introduced a handsome serviceman stationed at Kirtland Air Base in Albuquerque to her family and, of course, to the church. This afternoon Lance had married the couple who now shook hands and hugged the friends and family overflowing the room.

Zach ran back and forth determined to see that every teenage girl in the room had a glass of punch. On the other hand Gayle made a determined effort to refuse an offer of a slice of cake from each teenage male who offered. "I'm afraid I've gained too much. I don't look fat to you, do I?" Most of the boys in the room had been given the opportunity to comment on her figure.

Lance made it his goal to talk to as many people as possible while focusing on the groom's parents. They were from the Texas

Hill Country and lived near the community where Lance had begun his pastoral ministry.

Willow took her role as Minister's wife quite seriously. She specifically looked for anyone who might appear to be alone or uncomfortable. At a wedding reception you don't expect to find many wallflowers but no matter what the gathering there was always at least one who experienced the abandoned shipwreck syndrome. A twelve-year old named Sylvia filled that role. Her mother, a friend of the bride's parents, rushed between the kitchen and the refreshment tables leaving no time for attention to her daughter. Sylvia probably would become a beautiful adult but presently limped through an ugly duckling stage. Having next to no social skills she pushed away any friendships. Willow frequently found Sylvia alone in church activities and was not surprised to discover this was the case this afternoon.

"What did you think of the bridesmaids' dresses?" she asked, recognizing Sylvia sewed her own clothes more from a need to save money than an interest in dress designing.

Sylvia shrugged. "A little gaudy."

"They usually are. You know nobody ever wears bridesmaid dresses after the wedding."

"Why do they make them so awful then? That just isn't practical."

Willow laughed and then commented on Sylvia's dress. From there they talked about life outside the wedding reception.

After a bit two women, Jacqueline and Abigail pulled Willow away from Sylvia. Jackie and Abby enjoyed the advantage of being stay at home housewives because both of their husbands were quite successful in what they did. The advantage for FLPC was having two women contributing considerable volunteer time to the church. Feminine volunteer work built American houses of worship since colonial times but in the modern era churches and synagogues have lost much of that free contribution since with the increase of women's employment came the decrease of women's free time. Both of these women had served as hostesses for this reception. Now they were taking a break to satisfy their curiosity.

"What on earth did Jennifer do?" Jackie spit out a harsh whisper.

"What have you heard?" Willow cautiously replied.

"Nothing very definitive," said Abby. "Just the vague comment that Zinnia's death was suspicious."

"Suspicious how?"

"Maybe she was given an overdose of something?" Jackie looked around and turned so her back was more toward the reception crowd.

"Well," said Willow forcefully, "all you've heard are vague innuendos. I know Jennifer - she's like my sister. And she would not do anything inappropriate, unethical, immoral, illegal, or wrong."

"Okay, okay. We were just asking," said Jackie.

Abby put her hands up and nodded vigorously.

"Anything we can do?" asked Jackie.

"Change the subject," said Willow.

"Excuse me?"

"When someone says anything about Jennifer just politely take the conversation in a different direction."

Jackie and Abby looked at one another.

"What if they bring it back up?" said Jackie.

"Then you can very forcefully say you don't believe in gossip."

"Okay," said Abby, "maybe we don't believe in it but some people live by it."

Jackie nodded her head vigorously.

Zinnia answered the knock at her door with an invitation to come in. Willow Carroll appeared around the door immediately followed by Lance. Zinnia lay in her bed with a copy of *To Kill a Mockingbird* by her side.

"Come in. Come in," she waved to them.

"How are you, Zinnia," Willow asked.

"Fine right at the minute. Nurse Jennifer was here about half an hour ago. She says the two of you work together."

"That's right and she's one of the best. She will treat you right."

"Oh, I'm convinced of that. Why don't you both sit."

"Oh no," said Lance. "We're just here for a quick hello and to check on you."

"And I want you to know," said Willow, "my husband has a great bed-side manner. Please call on him for anything you need."

"I will."

"I mean it. He can't help you medically, but spiritually, he's the best."

"I'm going to remember that," Zinnia said. "I'll certainly remember that."

Willow looked across the room at Lance listening intently to an older woman explaining or complaining or enlisting his support for some cause. His eyes focused on her face. His tight mouth suggested he was taking every word of her argument to heart. His shoulders bent toward her. Suddenly Willow remembered the evening he returned home to report his latest visit with Zinnia Foster. She was certain he had shown Zinnia the same intense posture of listening. She could almost hear their conversation.

Lance: "Zinnia, you must understand I want to be by your side any time and every time you need me."

Zinnia: "I know that. And I want you to know I appreciate it. But you know, Lance, sometimes I can't bear to see you or Jennifer come into my room."

Willow remembered Lance describing the shock he felt when Zinnia told him this. She seemed to remember he went on to tell her Zinnia started to cry at that point.

Lance: "Zinnia, can you tell me more about this?"

Zinnia: "Oh, I can't make sense any more. It just hurts so much and all the time. And I see it in your faces. You hurt for me. I love you both for that but that just makes it hurt all the more."

Lance: (Who was probably fighting tears himself,) "I'm sorry."

Zinnia: "How much longer Lance? How much longer?"

Willow didn't know how the conversation went from there. That was the extent of what he had told her that evening.

"Willow?" Jackie said.

Willow shivered and gave her friends a weak smile.

Jackie touched her arm. "We lost you for a second there."

"Sorry. My mind just, ah, well let's join the party.

Jackie and Abby quickly agreed and moved away.

Willow took a minute to speculate about what her husband and Zinnia might have said to one another. A bizarre notion skipped across the back of her mind. She shook her head and went in search of anyone who could distract her.

Gayle, Rosita, and Nancy, Las Tres Amigas, rode their bikes down a street that led to an actual island in Rio Rancho. A developer had ringed his housing with ponds making them appear to be set on an island. The girls had been curious about the area and decided they would check it out. Gayle and Nancy covered their heads with their hoodies. Rosita wore a watch cap. The cool, clear autumn day required some such protection against the breeze.

"Just typical Rio Raunch," sniffed Nancy.

"No, I like it," objected Rosita.

Both looked to Gayle for her assessment.

"S'alright," she said with a gravelly voice. The other two laughed.

"Nice biking wear," Rosita said to Gayle.

Nancy glanced at Gayle's spandex biking trunks, "You didn't wear that to the reception I hope." At that Rosita and Gayle laughed.

Gayle waved at the pond in front of them and asked, "What were you expecting."

"Wasn't expecting anything," said Nancy. "I just wanted to see what was here.

Rosita giggled.

"What? What did I say?"

"Well, I don't mean to be picky. But you are expecting."

All three laughed at that and Gayle declared she would have to tell her father that Rosita had come up with a halfway decent pun.

"No, don't tell him. I'm not ready for anyone to know."

Gayle got off her bike. They had been sitting the bikes, one foot for balance on the ground. Gayle turned hers and began to walk back the way they had come.

Nancy rushed to catch up. "You haven't told him about me, have you?" After a pause she continued, "You have! You told him."

Gayle stopped walking. "I haven't told him about you. I, uh, I simply raised a hypothetical question about what options would someone have if someone were pregnant."

Nancy let her bike drop by the side of the road. "Oh, I can't believe this. You know I didn't want anyone to know. You told him!"

"No I didn't. I never mentioned your name. I never said you were pregnant." She pointed at Nancy for emphasis.

Rosita had lagged behind but not so much that she couldn't hear the conversation. She obviously was uncomfortable with the building disagreement between her friends.

"I know you don't want people to know yet, but we need help from some mature, experienced minds."

"We can get that later. Right now I don't want anyone to know."

Rosita set the kickstand and balanced her bike on the asphalt. Then she picked up Nancy's bike and did the same for it. "How far along are you Nance? People are going to start guessing pretty soon."

"Yeah," agreed Gayle. "I think I can already detect a bump. I wouldn't think anything about it today if I didn't already know. But maybe next week. Or soon anyway."

Nancy's eyes widened. A frown darkened her face. "Really?" She absent-mindedly rubbed her belly.

Rosita pushed an arm across her shoulders.

Nancy rubbed her face with both hands.

"So, what did your father have to say?"

"Ugh!" Gayle groaned.

"Come on," encouraged Rosita. "Be helpful here."

"Well, apparently our choices are," she counted on her fingers, "Not Good, Bad, Worse, and Truly Awful."

Rosita leaned toward Gayle and hissed, "What part of 'Be helpful here' did you not understand."

"I'm just trying to be honest."

Gayle pushed her bicycle out of the street to avoid a pickup driving by.

"Start with the truly awful," said Nancy. "Let's get that out of the way."

"Abortion."

"No way," said Rosita.

"I'm not going to hell over this," said Nancy.

"That's your priest speaking. My dad doesn't agree with that. But, yeah, that's the most evil choice."

"Next."

"Get married."

"No!" shouted Rosita.

Nancy just laughed - a derisive snort. "That's a pretty evil choice."

"Okay, moving on. You can either give the baby up for adoption or you can raise your child as a single mother."

"What else?" asked Rosita.

"Nothing else. There's no fairy godmother going to sprinkle whiffle dust on your belly and make it all better. These are pretty much our choices."

"Yeah," nodded Nancy. "I've pretty much gone over all of those." She turned toward her bike, kicked up the stand, and started pushing it up the street.

"Did you notice Gayle's use of the plural?"

Nancy stopped and turned around. "Huh?"

"Gayle kept saying 'our' choices. Even if you don't want anyone else to know, we know. We're with you Nance."

Quietly Nancy said, "I know that."

Lance retrieved the day's mail from the curb-side mailbox just as Gayle arrived on her bike.

"Anything for me?"

"Probably. We get tons of mail but only the bills have my name on them." After a moment of thumbing through the envelopes Lance shook his head. "Nope, nothing this time." He smiled at his daughter. "Been out with your friends?"

Gayle threw her leg high in the air to dismount her bike and Lance chuckled.

"Something funny?"

"Youth. No, not funny. More amazing than amusing."

She frowned. "What?"

"Never mind." He turned toward the garage walking with Gayle as she put away her bike.

"So, what's up with the ladies today?"

"We went exploring." She leaned against Lance's work table, apparently not yet ready to go into the house.

"Exploring Rio Rancho? Doesn't sound too exciting."

"Exciting? Maybe not but it can be interesting." She hesitated. "We talked about, you know, our options."

"Your options?"

"Yeah, remember I asked you what choices a pregnant teen has ..."

"Oh, right. Any decisions?"

181

"Of course not. We're just not ready for decisions yet."

"We ... have you taken over the responsibility for this baby? May I remind you that you told me someone else, not you, is pregnant?"

"She can't do this by herself."

"Oh absolutely. She needs support. And I have no doubt you are a wonderful friend. But, what about her family? Do her parents know about this?"

"Not yet. Pretty soon everyone will know. She's in her last days of being able to keep it secret. But, no, only the three of us know right now."

"Do you have an idea about how the parents will react?"

"I do." She turned around and opened Lance's tool box, fiddling with screwdrivers. "You never know for sure until something actually happens. But I'm pretty sure they will overreact and go all melodramatic on her."

"Melodramatic. Of course they will have a serious emotional reaction. Chances are pretty good they are not aware their daughter is sexually active. ..."

"That's true."

"So the possibility that she is pregnant ... Well, of course."

"I know Dad. Any set of parents would have some shock and whatever, but Nan ... uh, my friend's parents are kind of out on the edge here." Gayle looked up at Lance, a question clearly on her face.

"I didn't hear you say her name."

"I don't mind telling you but I need to be able to tell her that I haven't betrayed her confidence."

"You haven't." He hugged her. "You're a great friend."

Zinnia's Girls Memorial Service at the Ladies of Charity House

The Ladies of Charity House, the facility built by Zinnia and her friends included a comfortable parlor that made a perfect setting for the Zinnia's Girls Memorial Service. Once again Lance found himself presiding over a time of remembrance for a dear lady. In only slightly less formal a setting than the Mi Casa service, he still stood at the front of the room with no podium.

"I'm Lance Carroll, Miss Zinnia's pastor. Don't get nervous. I'm not going to preach a sermon. I simply want to thank you for coming and I want to give you a chance to say something about Miss Zinnia. You are welcome to say whatever you want about your memories of her. And, if this bothers you, you are welcome just to listen to whatever other people want to say. You don't have to talk. Let me start by telling you what she told me about you.

"One day I asked her, 'Miss Zinnia, how goes it with the Ladies of Charity House?' She told me, 'This is the hardest work and the most fun I have ever had.' How about that? 'Hard work and fun at the same time?' I asked. 'Not always at the same time,' she told me. She explained, 'The hard part is convincing these young women they are beautiful and wonderful. The fun is watching them learn that I am telling them the truth.'

"So, there you have the word of Miss Zinnia. You young ladies are beautiful and wonderful. Now who wants to say something about Miss Zinnia?"

Chapter Fourteen

Lance looked over his congregation and scratched his head. "I guess what I'm intending to say is this: Ask probing questions but be suspicious of quick answers.

"Let me illustrate this way." He waved a hand as though introducing someone.

"The Jews enjoyed a rather elastic understanding of theology. Rabbi Hillel - some of you recognize that name because the Jewish student center at UNM is named for him - Hillel said 'If I am not for myself, then who will be for me? But if I am only for myself, what am I?' A contemporary, Rabbi Shammai, sometimes disagreed with Hillel. Shammai was more strict in his understanding of Jewish law. Hillel was more liberal. But, note this, Jewish sages declared both their positions were equally valid. These men lived about a generation before Jesus."

Someone stood from a place in the back of the congregation and left the sanctuary. Lance lost his train of thought for a moment but then continued.

"When the Christians came along one of the first big controversies was over the question, 'Do we have to become a Jew before we can be a Christian?' Good question. Not one any of us would ask today, but a good question none the less." Lance surveyed the congregation as though searching for disagreement."

A child spoke up, not where Lance could understand what was said. A parent made a shushing noise.

"Eventually the orthodox answer became, 'No. We don't have to be Jews.' I'm okay with that as a generality. But as a written-in-stone, orthodox position it has problems. An early Christian leader declared Christians do not need the Old Testament. Many Christians fail to understand the Jewish background of Jesus and the disciples. Christian history is rife with anti-Semitism. So the question is better than the orthodox answer. We don't have to become Jews but we can't ignore our Jewish connection."

Whoever had left the congregation earlier returned to his place. Probably a bathroom trip, Lance thought.

"Other good questions causing debate in the early church were, 'How do you describe the Trinity?' and 'Please explain how Jesus is both Man and God.' Great questions stimulating wonderful debates. But once official, orthodox answers were announced, Christianity fractured and 'heretic' became a curse-word."

At about that point Lance noticed an increased level of fidgeting and coughing. He had learned a long time earlier that there is no good way to rescue a sermon only the preacher loves other than to just shut up and sit down. So he did so - after a summary statement that he hoped everyone would continue to ask great questions.

One crisp day when it became clear summer was at an end Sally Ingersoll introduced Jennifer Garcia to Zinnia explaining that Jennifer was a nurse and might have some helpful information for Zinnia. At that point Zinnia had moved from her home to a hospital bed and then into Mi Casa. The first thing Zinnia said was, "I don't know if anyone can help me."

Jennifer opened her eyes wide and said, "Try me."

Zinnia looked the nurse up and down, nodded, pursed her lips, nodded again and said, "The doctor tells me it's stage four. I demand straightforwardness and he complies. He did what he could." She sniffed. "Bless his heart. You know, he so wanted to do this for me. I think it broke his heart when Mr. Foster died. Well," she waved her hand as if erasing difficult memories. "What do you expect when all your patients are old so-and-sos like Mr. Foster and me?"

She grimaced and rolled her body into herself as though retreating to a fetal position.

"Are you hurting?" asked Jennifer.

Zinnia partially straightened. She sat in one of the two comfortable chairs in her room, her rocking chair. After Sally had left the two of them to talk Jennifer had sat opposite Zinnia in the other chair. She leaned forward and lightly touched Zinnia's hand. "Has anything helped?"

Zinnia pulled a tissue from the box by her side and wiped her eyes.

"No." The softness of her answer surprised Jennifer some. Until then Zinnia's voice had been quite school-teachery strong. "Nothing helps and the pain is getting worse." She looked up at the nurse with an expression saying, "I told you, you couldn't help."

"Well, Zinnia, maybe nothing can be done but let me tell you who I am and what I do. I'm a hospice nurse. We help people make their last journey. We mainly provide palliative care."

"You keep them comfortable."

"Ah, you know what palliative means."

"I have developed an extensive vocabulary."

"Of course you have. We're realists, you and I. We both know every problem can't be solved. But since hospice focuses on comfort rather than cures, we do know a lot about pain management."

"That's encouraging."

"As a matter of fact, your doctor put me on to you. Did he suggest you might be expecting me?"

"We haven't talked for several days. The last time I saw him I got the impression it was just too hard on him so ... well, Jennifer, I just decided not to go back."

"Dear Zinnia. Too busy caring for others to take care of yourself."

"Well, I'm thinking we, you and I, might just get along. But I have a concern."

"Okay. What's your concern?"

"You're not going to want to keep me past my 'use-by date', are you?"

"Excuse me?"

"You know, milk, or whatever's in the fridge, has a date when it's time to throw it out. Some people don't have enough sense to know when time's up."

Jennifer touched Zinnia's arm. "I think I understand what you are saying, Zinnia. But you are not something to be discarded."

Zinnia smiled and moved her hand to take Jennifer's in hers.

"Thank you for that. I wasn't thinking about being discarded. That's not a pleasant picture. But release? Yes, release. I like that. Would you be willing to release me?"

Jennifer looked carefully at her new patient. "I think I really like you Zinnia. And that makes that an extremely important and terribly difficult question."

That visit was the first of several. For a time, much too brief, Jennifer kept Zinnia free of pain. Unfortunately when Zinnia was consuming enough painkiller to fell an elephant, it no longer helped.

191

"We have got to do something!" Willow marched around the kitchen yanking clean dishes and utensils from the dishwasher and slamming them into cabinets and drawers. Lance did his best to stay out of the line of fire.

"Maybe the best way to handle rumors is to ignore them. Let them die of their own accord," he offered.

"Really! Because this rumor is damaging to my hospice's reputation."

"So who's talking? What are they saying? You know everything seems so vague and unspecified. Is there any real substance to attack?"

Willow stopped her frantic dance for a moment and glared at Lance. "Jennifer's name keeps coming up. That's what really chaps me. The hospice can probably face this down, but she might lose her job if we can't put a stop to this."

Her face blanked for a moment.

"What are you thinking," Lance said.

"You know, losing her job might not be the worst thing that could happen to her."

"Oh?"

"No. What if she were arrested?"

"Ah, come on. That's not going to happen."

"Really? Well I know she's not guilty of anything. I mean it would never go to trial or anything like that. But just being taken to a police station for questioning could be all it would take to destroy her career."

"You can't really believe ..." He looked over her shoulder at his teen-agers.

"Mom, are you breaking things?" Gayle slipped into the kitchen followed closely by Zach wearing a frown.

"Getting some aerobic exercise. Are you going to see Rosita and Nancy today?"

"Maybe later. Nancy can't make up her mind. She wants to stay home." Gayle flipped her hands back and forth. "She doesn't want to stay home." Pointing at her mother she said, "Dad, do try to keep her calm. I want to do some homework." With that she twirled and disappeared down the hall.

Zach watched her depart and then turned toward his dad.

"Where'd you get the idea for that sermon today?"

"Oh, I was trying to use a lectionary text. I've never preached on it before."

"I can see why." He turned and quickly vanished into his room.

Lance shrugged. "That was helpful."

He moved to the stove turning on the burner beneath the teakettle. "Let's have some tea and talk about this calmly. For the sake of the children."

"Yeah, right, the children."

Lance pulled a pair of cups from the cabinet and fished around in another cabinet for a peach-mango tea bag. Within minutes they were seated at the kitchen table inhaling the fruity perfume from their mugs of tea.

"Would you be open to a couple of suggestions?" he wondered.

"Sure, I always want to know what you are thinking."

"So you can explain how I don't know what I'm talking about."

"Of course. But you once had a good idea."

"Oh? When was that?"

"Actually I'm just guessing. But it does seem possible."

Willow slurped a swallow of tea then held her cup in her hands enjoying its warmth. "So suggest away."

"All right. I'm thinking let's take the 'we' out of 'we have got to do something.' "

She frowned. "You're bailing out?"

"No, but I think you should. I'm afraid any energy you give to this will simply make it look more suspicious for the hospice. It probably won't do anything to help Jennifer."

Willow frowned some more but nodded her head.

"I, uh, I can't just ignore what's happening."

"Oh, I thought I got a 'yes' signal there for a minute."

She put her cup on the table.

"I'm really upset right now."

"I know you are."

"So what are you going to do, Captain America?"

"I know Mi Casa's administrator about as well as you or Jennifer do. I'll pay her a call. See what I can learn. Maybe make a suggestion."

Willow turned in her chair and retrieved her cup again. "I'm not encouraged, but then, it beats anything I can think of."

She rose and returned, a bit more calmly, to straightening her kitchen. Lance thought about his son's comment and retraced his Sunday morning. He had planned a series of sermons following the scripture readings set out in the Common Lectionary used by

Presbyterians and others. His thought had
been to use texts that he had avoided in the
past because they were obscure or
problematic in some way. Not a bad idea, he
realized, if he had put his best thinking to
the task. But this morning he couldn't
concentrate on what he wanted to say. All he
could do was revisit conversations with
Zinnia Foster.

"You know, Mr. Foster was by far the
best friend I ever had," she had told him
once. He was amused by the habit of older
people to refer to their spouses formally. She
always spoke of her husband as "Mr. Foster"
never using his given name. Lance thought
about that for a moment and realized he
couldn't remember his given name. The
main point of that particular conversation
centered on her husband's ability to find the
right solution to any problem she had. And,
if he had not "pre-deceased" her - she felt
that was a stupid term made up by insurance
underwriters - if he were still alive, he
would know how to help her move on past
her pain. Wendell - that was his name. Did
anyone ever call her Mrs. Wendell Foster?

No, she was Zinnia or Miss Zinnia, an individual in her own right. No wonder he couldn't remember Wendell's name. No one ever said it.

Willow touched his shoulder. "Are you stewing about Zach's comment?"

"Huh?"

"I know you sometimes get sensitive when church people miss the point of your sermon."

"No, no, I'm not stewing about Zach. He was right. That wasn't my best effort this morning."

"Uh-huh. Well, I'm glad you recognized that."

Lance looked up at her. "Thank you very much."

"Thank you, Patrick. Thank you very much."

Patrick served as Lance's sounding board all during his ministry in San Marcos. They began a friendship when Lance sat next to Patrick during lunch at a Presbytery meeting soon after Lance's initial pastorate had begun. Walking outside for a break before the afternoon session, Patrick asked him how things were going in Lance's part of the Presbyterian Patch.

Lance welcomed the question. Patrick was also a young minister, but had a few years' experience behind him, so Lance felt both kinship and confidence.

"I dunno," Lance said. "I had a counseling session I'm not really sure about."

"You were the counselor, not the counselled."

"That's right."

"What part of it poses a problem?"

"Well, the couple wanted an abortion ... They've already gotten the abortion, I imagine."

"What did they want from you?"

"They said they wanted advice about coming clean with their parents."

"Umm. Not sure how you advise someone on that."

"Yeah. That's what I thought. I really think what they wanted was a get-out-of-jail-free pass. They wanted me to go all 'Ego absolvo te.' "

"Catholic absolution."

"Something like that."

"And we don't do that, but it doesn't matter, people still want the preacher's permission."

"So, what should I have done?"

"Who knows? Who cares?"

"We care. We may not know but we care."

"Of course you care. That's why this is bugging you. But in a real, wide-world-of-sports sense it doesn't matter. Much of the time people have made up their minds what they are going to do and it does not matter what you say or do."

"I just don't like feeling I was complicit in their securing an abortion."

Patrick poked Lance's chest. "Now don't try to guilt yourself over this. I remind you again we are not Catholics. Abortion is not necessarily a sin."

"Yeah, I get that. But selfishness is."

Zinnia's Girls Memorial Service at the Ladies of Charity House

After a few seconds of nervous giggling a young woman stood.

"Hi. My name is Alicia and I got pregnant when I shouldna done it. Everyone talks about pregnancy like it is the start of a new life, and it is, it is. But I thought, you know, my life is over. It's done, at least I thought so. I thought my Mom hated me. I don't believe that now but it sure felt that way at the time. I had to drop out of school, lost contact with all my friends. My boyfriend said it was my fault. I should have done something about it. I didn't know what I could have done. Yeah I know about birth control now, but not then. I know one thing I can do now. I'm not ever seeing him again. But, anyway, I was sure everything was all over for me. Then I found out about the Ladies of Charity and Miss Zinnia. She helped me earn my GED, she helped me learn how to be a friend so I could earn friends, and she taught me how to walk into the future. 'Learn from your past but leave it behind you,' she said. Turns out my life just got started after my pregnancy. It didn't end."

Chapter Fifteen

A middle-aged couple walked into Mi Casa's cafeteria followed by Sally Ingersoll rolling a wheelchair ensconced elderly woman. The man inspected every bit of the room with a serious frown. His wife, wearing a satisfied smile, took in the vibrant colors, comfortable furniture and the smells of lunch being prepared.

"So I think you can see, Hannah and Walter that Mary Beth can be quite happy living here with us."

"Oh I believe so," said Hannah.

Walter interrupted his scanning of the room to nod his head. He bent toward the wheelchair. "What do you think Mom?"

Mary Beth lifted her head chirping a small laugh. "Did you say they have a swimming pool?"

"No, they don't have one Mom, but maybe we could drive down to the lake occasionally."

"That would be nice Walter."

"I think you'd love it here Mom," offered Hannah.

"As long as Trixie can come with me."

Walter straightened up and muttered, "Hmm. Well Trixie's not with us anymore."

Sally moved the wheelchair to one of the tables. "I believe you folks are planning to eat lunch here today. Put us to the test, if you will."

She waved forward a man in a white smock and introduced the cook followed by kitchen staff members. After instructing the staff to take good care of Mary Beth she reminded Walter and Hannah to stop by her office after their meal. She then headed back down the hall.

She no sooner entered her secretary's office than Lance Carroll walked in behind her.

"Reverend Carroll, how good to see you. You know you show up here so often we may have to declare you the Mi Casa chaplain."

"Nice to see you, Ms. Ingersoll."

"Haven't you been in New Mexico long enough to know first names are all the formality we allow?"

"Whoa, now listen, you Reverended me."

"Oh that's right, I did. Shame on me. Well, Lance, what can I do for you?"

"Can you spare me about two minutes?"

"Surely. Come in my office. Coffee?"

"No, thank you. Just conversation."

Sally motioned Lance to a sofa against one wall of the office and then settled herself in a matching chair nearby. She asked about Willow and the kids. Lance made some appropriate comments and then addressed his reason for visiting.

"I'm concerned about what official statement will be made relative to Zinnia Foster's death."

Lance was aware of a grand silence descending on the room. Sally seemed to compose herself for a moment before responding.

The administrator smiled, crossed her legs and folded her hands. "You have a concern."

Lance swallowed, adjusted his tie, and wondered just how much he had overstepped some boundary. "Ah, yes. Maybe just a little more than idle curiosity."

"Lance you were Zinnia's pastor. You are also, as far as I'm concerned, a friend of our facility."

Lance nodded.

"Anyone else who is not family, physician, or Mi Casa staff who would raise a question like that would be courteously told ..."

"To mind your own business," interrupted Lance.

"Succinctly put." She waved her hand as if to clear away whatever tension had been created. "Tell me what's bothering you."

Lance accepted her invitation to comment.

"I'm hearing gossip that is a disservice to Zinnia's memory, and, well, uh also the reputation of the hospice program that served her, and, frankly, it doesn't help Mi Casa."

"And do you know the source of this gossip?"

"No, I don't."

"I see. Well, of course, I'll look into it and if you learn any specifics, I'd like to know about it."

"Sally, I hope you see me as an ally rather than an adversary."

"From Day One, Lance."

Lance smiled, stood, and offered his hand. "Thank you, Sally."

She stood and shook hands with him. "And just so you know, Zinnia officially died of natural causes."

"Of course she did," Lance said.

♥ ♥ ♥ ♥

"Did you ever read the novel *Shogun*?"

Lance glanced at the ceiling. "Long time ago." Looking back at Zinnia he wrinkled his brow, "Why?"

"Do you remember that young Japanese girl who decides life is too, I don't know, too twisted."

"Well the story is rather fuzzy in my mind. Doesn't she commit suicide?"

"Well, more than suicide, seppuku, an honorable death. It's a very complicated story. She's the wife of a brutal Samurai; she loves the main character, a European sailor, she's an agent for the Japanese warlord who plots to become Shogun."

Lance leaned toward her, "Ah-huh ..."

"Clavell does a brilliant job of describing that whole experience. You feel that she was courageous and possessed a great strength of mind to be able to go through that experience."

"Did she kill herself or was she murdered?"

"She intended, at one point to kill herself. If I remember correctly, that's increasingly a problem for me, she allowed herself to be killed as an act of seppuku."

Resting his face in his hands Lance stared at her.

"I asked Lucinda to find me a copy of that book but she never did. She said it wasn't in that dinky library they have here. I wanted to read that one chapter again. I've just always thought of that young woman as a tragic heroine. No one wants to be in that position. But if you are ... so many questions, so many different strengths are required."

"Oh?" Lance was desperately trying keep up.

"Do you know how hopeless the current path is?"

"But ..."

"Do you really see how limited your options?"

"Well ..."

"Are you going to make the hard choices or are you going to give up and let others ..." She coughed several times and Lance jumped up to hand her a glass of water. She drank, handed him the glass and waved for him to sit, indicating he was just to listen.

"If you leave the hard questions and decisions to others, they may very well with the best of intentions make the worst decisions."

"Not necessarily."

"Have you got the will power, the courage to say 'I am going to stay in charge of my own life'?"

Recognizing this was no longer a conversation, Lance decided to lean back and let Zinnia continue.

"Maybe she didn't make the best decision or the right decision, but it was her decision. Her life. Her decision."

Zinnia remained quiet. A tear leaked from one eye.

Lance leaned forward, nodded. "I heard you."

As Lucinda returned to her desk she found Mr. Reaves awaiting her.

"Afternoon Mr. Reaves. How are you?"

"A little embarrassed, ah," he glanced at the name plate on the desk, "Ms. Dominguez."

"Oh, surely not. What about?"

"I told my wife about that last conversation we had, where I kind of tweaked you about suspicious deaths."

"Uh-huh."

"She said I was rude."

"Oh, not at all."

"Yes. She said I was rude - which is just my natural state, by the way - and maybe you had a serious concern. Anyway," he flapped a hand. "I came to see Mom and thought I'd stop and apologize."

"No need, really, no need." Lucinda twisted one way and then the other and finally sat.

"Well, I'll be off to check on Mom. But if there's ever anything you need to tell me about, I'm available."

"Oh," she squeaked and pulled out a drawer hoping to find something to do as Mr. Reaves walked off.

Willow packed away her stethoscope and blood pressure cuff then turned to smile at Mr. Haley.

"When you're going downhill," he rasped, "you pick up speed."

"As long as you are not hurting, Mr. H. That's my chief concern."

"Thanks for that, Nurse Willow." With that he started a coughing fit.

Willow sat down in the wicker chair by the bed an placed a hand on his shoulder.

After a moment the coughing subsided and he closed his eyes. She patted his shoulder and left the room. In the hallway outside his room Mrs. Haley waited with a questioning expression on her face. Willow took her arm and they walked into the living room of the Haley's apartment.

"I think he's got more days in him, but the signs the doctor described to you are progressing. Fortunately we have been able to keep him fairly comfortable. I hope that continues."

They talked about a next visit for Willow and then she left.

In the car she realized she was not far from the Klepner's parsonage so she decided to drop in on Dorothy to see how she was doing.

Dorothy met her at the door with a big smile.

"Surprise! I just thought I would see what The Real Housewife of Albuquerque is doing."

"Ha," Dorothy laughed, "the TV crew just left. Watch for the latest episode next summer."

"Can't wait."

"Come in. Let's get some coffee in us. What are you doing in my neighborhood?"

Willow followed Dorothy to her kitchen.

"Just did a visit with a hospice patient and realized I'd almost drive past your house on the way back to the office so I thought, why not see Dorothy?"

The two women arranged themselves on stools at a worktable and surveyed plants and pictures, calendars and recipes and whatever else Willow's eyes captured.

Then Dorothy said, "Got a question for you."

"Okay, what?"

"Who are you?"

"What?" Willow's response slid upward through an octave.

"Well, of course, everybody knows who Willow Carroll is. But what I'd like to know is: Do you have any problem knowing who you are?"

"Ah, gee, I mean, now there's a question for you."

"Really, I know it. But I'm serious. See, you just came from a patient. I would guess this patient isn't long for this world and you are making a big difference in how he ... I guess I should say 'or she' shouldn't I."

"He - this time."

"Okay, he will part this world in a little better shape because you are a part of his last days."

"I hope that's true. I'm not always sure of that."

"You do a good job. I have no doubt of that."

"Thank you."

"More coffee?"

Willow waved her off. "No. I'm fine."

Dorothy got up to refill her own cup.

"What are you looking for," Willow said.

Dorothy returned to her seat.

"You're an efficient hospice nurse, the mother of two brilliant children - young people - and a minister's wife."

"Uh-huh."

"Right now I'm just a minister's wife. Don't get me wrong. I love my husband. I'm glad he's doing something meaningful for him. I love my kids. But they're out of the house. And so is he pretty much. He finds meaning in his church. I don't."

"What do you mean by that?"

"Nothing heretical. I'm not having any crisis of faith right here. I'm just - well, kind of empty. Actually a crisis might be exciting. I'm just bored."

"I don't know Dorothy. Some days boring sounds good. You know I think it's a Chinese curse rather than a blessing, 'May you live in interesting times.' "

"What would you say if I suggested reading *Fifty Shades of Grey*?"

Both women laughed and then Willow tried to decide whether she thought Dorothy was serious or not.

After more conversation and a little more coffee Willow drove away trying to decipher her feelings about what Dorothy had said. She was a nursing student when she first met Pastor Lance. Throughout her marriage she had thought of herself as a nurse. That was her identity. She became a wife and then a mother. Both of those roles required some alterations in her nursing career. She really hadn't given a lot of thought to what Lance's vocation meant to her identity. She is a nurse, that's what she does. He is a minister, that's what he does. They happen to be married. That makes her a preacher's wife. And he is a nurse's husband. Hmm, she thought. Never heard him described like that.

"Young man, I don't think you are listening to me."

Robert Underhill was chairman of the Presbytery's committee that supervised the relationships between pastors and churches in the Texas Hill Country about a decade before the great 2K change in the calendar.

Lance and the Reverend Underhill were standing behind Lance's church, next to a large garbage can. Underhill had suggested they come outside for a conversation that might not be appropriate for some of the parishioners doing janitorial duties to hear. In Lance's mind the Presbyterian official had ambushed him in the middle of a very congenial congregational work day.

Once outside Underhill told Lance that he had learned that the young pastor was telling college students not to worry about sexual activities because they could always get an abortion. Later Lance cornered Patrick who explained he was trying to get help for Lance, encouragement in his role as a Christian counselor. Whatever Patrick thought about it. Underhill saw his responsibility toward Reverend Carroll quite differently.

Lance tried to explain. "I wasn't white-washing sexual dalliance ..."

"This could permanently mark your ministry in a profoundly negative way." Underhill had no interest in anything Lance wanted to say.

It'll go on my permanent record, thought Lance, and he had to restrain a laugh.

Actually it could have been a career breaker except that Underhill had some difficulties with his own congregation and eventually left Texas for the New England area. Lance never heard from him again. But there were still times when he would wake from a dream hearing the words, "Young man, I don't think you are listening to me."

Thinking about Robert Underhill reminded him of a woman in San Marcos who frequently appeared before the city's school board, decrying the teaching of sex education in the public schools. Both of her daughters had abortions while in high school.

Zinnia's Girls Memorial Service at the Ladies of Charity House

Alicia was followed quickly by another woman who appeared to be a twenties-something.

"I'm Christy. I don't know the SOB who got me pregnant. Never saw him before and haven't seen him since. I was very opposed to abortion. Still am. But I couldn't bear to bring a child into the world whose daddy did things like that to girls. I couldn't. Miss Zinnia agreed with me that abortion was basically wrong. I guess that was my first surprise when I came here. Yeah, it's wrong but there are other wrongs in life. She told me once, 'If you are mired in mud, you need to get out. But you're not going to right away step from mud to grass. You've got more mud to tromp through before you leave it completely.' That man should not leave children in the world. By the way Miss Zinnia taught me to quit calling him - well, you can figure that part out. The rest of my life isn't about him. So I don't waste my time or energy on him. I'm getting well. It'll take a long time. But, thanks to Miss Zinnia, I'm better."

Albuquerque Journal
Editorial
January 17, 2015
Appeal Ruling, Amend Law on
Assisting Suicide
... it should not be up to the courts to
decide which patients die, which don't, and
how it's done."

Chapter Sixteen

The sun shone brilliantly over the golf course. A bright azure sky highlighted the Sandias. A slight breeze rippled the flags at each hole.

Mac bent over and rubbed his hand across the grass of the first green. "Super dry year. It takes its toll on the golf courses."

"And on the golfers," said Benny.

Lance placed a marker so he could pick up his ball. "Am I the only one on the green in regulation?"

"If by regulation you mean five strokes not counting penalties, we all reached the green in regulation."

Leonard wagged his bag up to Mac's golf cart. "Sorry I'm late," he panted.

"Parishioner counseling?" asked Benny.

"No." Leonard strapped his bag to the cart. "Roof leak in the janitor's closet. Big mess."

"Good thing you hired a janitor or you never would have found it."

Leonard yanked his putter out of the bag and threw a ball on the green. "Oh we never hired a janitor. Volunteers just like always. So, we all got here in five just like usual?"

"Yeah," the other three groused.

By the time they reached the clubhouse after the ninth hole they had collectively lost twenty-one balls, a new record for the Unholy Four. Relieved by the potty break and with new drinks in hand they settled at the tenth tee to watch two other groups who had taken advantage of their break to surge ahead.

Benny asked for news about Lance's ethical dilemma.

"You sure you want to know?"

"Ah yes," said Mac. "Should you do right or do good?"

"Who says what the correct answer should be?" asked Leonard.

Mac pointed at him. "Well, wait a minute. Who says who says?"

Benny laughed. "There's no end to that puppy chasing his tail."

"No, and no matter where you stop, you will not find an answer," said Lance.

Benny placed his hands together reverentially. "Right. What you Christians never understand is, this demonstrates the value of the Talmud. As you pursue one rabbi's reference to a previous rabbi's comments on another rabbi's analysis you get so dizzy chasing the impression that there *is* an answer to your question that you assume your failure to understand must be entirely your own fault."

"Huh?"

"See what I mean."

Lance explained to them that nothing unethical had occurred. There simply was an issue of gossip. "You see there's no real evidence of wrong doing but rumors can be destructive."

"Boy, you got that right." Leonard took off on a long narrative about malicious slander he experienced early in his ministry. Fortunately for the other three the tee box cleared and they had to get on with the business of losing golf balls.

When they reconvened at the next green Mac said, "I guess you decided against using the Catholic priest and nun story as an alternative rumor?"

"Oh, wow! Right! I forgot all about that little dodge. Thanks for reminding me, Mac."

"Me and my big mouth."

Leonard lined up his putt, being the furthest from the hole. He then putted two feet right of the hole and watched as his ball rolled off the green into a bunker.

Mac then putted into the same bunker. "Tell you what I'll do," he said as he pulled his sand wedge from his bag. "I'll teach you about casuistry. That may save your bacon."

Lance looked up from lining up his putt. "What's casuistry?"

"Case-based reasoning," answered Benny.

"Oh, now I'm getting a lecture in stereo."

"Jews and Catholics know about casuistry," said Benny.

On his second try Leonard hit his ball out of the sand trap and over the green. "Oh brother," he muttered.

"Don't let your play bother you," advised Lance.

"Oh that wasn't about my shot. I'm just not sure I want a Catholic-Jewish choreographed seminary lecture."

Lance's ball pretended to go in the hole, rimmed out and rolled five-feet down the green.

"No, no," said Mac, "this is just friendly advice. It'll help Larc."

"Lark?" said Benny. "Who's Lark?"

"Oh that's what I call him sometimes. Lance Ramsey Carroll - L-R-C, or L-A-R-K, if you like."

"How will it help me?"

"Well," said Benny, taking up the teaching role, "casuistry insists every incident is a separate case. Therefore you find all the arguments you can muster on the specific facts of that one event."

The crew loaded their putters in the bags and headed for the next tee.

"I dunno," said Mac, "maybe Catholic theology provides a better argument."

"Oh brother," Leonard repeated.

"Do you know the Doctrine of Double Effect?"

"Lance will become a Unitarian if this keeps up."

"No listen, this is good stuff. In any action there is both good and bad."

"Yeah, yeah, yeah," said Lance. "If you intend good and not the bad, then it's not your fault if the bad happens."

"Okay, it sounds better the way I tell it."

"The way you tell it takes longer and puts everybody to sleep," Benny said.

Leonard took off his ball-cap and wiped his forehead. "You guys are talking about that aid-in-dying stuff again, aren't you?"

"Don't miss a trick do you?" said Mac.

"Well, I'm telling you New Mexico law is a mess when it comes to this."

"Yeah," said Benny, "I saw something about that."

"Nobody knows what the law means," insisted Leonard, "and it keeps changing."

Lance stepped back from his golf cart. "The law changes or the interpretation of the law?"

"Both," Leonard paused. "I think."

In the parking lot, Lance closed his clubs in the back of his SUV and found Benny waiting at the driver's door.

"Need a ride some place?"

"No," said the rabbi, "just wanted to be sure you're all right before we part ways."

"Sure, I'm fine. Nice of you to ask."

"Really? Because I'm getting a vibe from you that says this is a huge problem that isn't going to just melt away in the New Mexican wind."

"Fancy another cola?"

Benny followed Lance to a fast food restaurant on Unser where they virtually had the place to themselves. Settled in a corner booth with soft drinks and a fried pie for

Benny, Lance watched traffic move on the Boulevard.

"It's getting to you, isn't it?"

"Well, there are implications."

"Implications?"

"Right. A good woman is dead. That was unavoidable. Her death was less painful than it might have been because someone cared. Maybe that's a big deal, but I don't think so. It is just done. It's over. Or it should be. But it isn't over if someone wants to paint it as something it is not."

"Back to the rumor problem."

Lance turned from the window to face Benny.

"Yeah, back to someone stirring up trouble when there doesn't have to be trouble."

Benny leaned on his elbows. "Let me play Devil's Advocate here."

"Oh surely you don't know anything about that?"

"You'd be surprised."

"Ha! Maybe I wouldn't."

Benny raised his eyebrows to which Lance waved him on.

"How do you know for certain that nothing evil transpired here?"

"What sort of evil could have transpired? This is a - what do they call it? - a locked room mystery?"

"I don't know. Is that a literary reference? I don't know anything about it."

"Yeah, well, never mind. Neither do I. But the point is, there are limited possibilities about what happened. She would have died very soon no matter what - no evil there but a considerable pain. So two possibilities: she died sooner, rather than later, of natural causes - God can be gracious and no evil there with much pain foreshortened. Or, possibly, she died sooner by medicinal causes - maybe a friend was gracious. I would claim no evil exists in the third scenario and, again, serious pain was eliminated."

"And if we leave it at that, no legal questions come up?"

"Maybe there are no legal questions at all. Leonard was right. New Mexico law is a little murky here. But the PR can be really damaging."

"PR for whom?"

"For the medical staff involved, for the facility where she died, for the hospice supervising her final days."

"Ah ha," said Benny leaning back, "family, friends and parishioners. All people dear to your heart."

Lance nodded as he returned his gaze to the traffic.

Lance answered the phone and listened to Victoria Roybal crying.

"Tell me what's going on Victoria."

"She's in such pain. The pills help some, but not much and not for long."

"I know, I know. And it cuts right to your heart, doesn't it."

"Isn't there something we can do? And don't tell me she's in God's hands and there's nothing we can do."

"All right. I won't tell you that if you'll give me a better response."

"I don't have one," she muttered.

"I'm sorry, Victoria. Neither do I."

The fact that no one in the family cared how Lance's golf excursion went did not stop him from describing in detail his magnificent drive on fourteen or the horrendous loss of a ball in a pond at eighteen when he was on the verge of winning the match. He was about to explain the intricacies of putting where the Sandia mountains and the Rio Grande river influenced the route of the ball when he realized Willow's somber expression overruled his golfing stories.

His pause allowed Zach and Gayle to escape into their rooms.

Frank seemed undecided about whether to stay with the parents or follow one of the siblings. As usual he chose Gayle's room.

Willow had sat at the kitchen table with chin in hands all through his recital. He now joined her there.

"What's going on?"

She raised her eyes toward him but otherwise did not move.

"Something more about Jennifer?"

"No. Not directly. Although what's bothering me I learned from her."

Lance waited for her to continue. Willow sat back in her chair and sighed.

"She went by Mi Casa this morning to do an intake on a new client. While she was there Ingersoll asked her if she knew anything about a pill bottle. Seems that

Lucinda - you know the receptionist don't you?"

"Oh yeah."

"Well, apparently she was in Zinnia's room immediately after she died and saw a bottle for a prescription pain reliever in the bedside table drawer. Why she was fishing around in Zinnia's room at that time is beyond me, but there she was. The prescription was dated within a week of Zinnia's death, but the bottle was almost empty."

"So who has the bottle?"

"No one. Nobody knows what happened to it."

"What was Sally asking Jennifer? Or, more to the point I guess, what did Jennifer say?"

"Ingersoll simply asked if Jennifer knew anything about it. Jennifer said she was aware of the prescription. She had given Zinnia pain medication quite frequently but as far as she knew the bottle was at the nurses' station."

"How could it have gotten into Zinnia's drawer?"

"Oh that's easy enough. Technically, if everything goes by procedure, it couldn't.

The bottle would never leave the nurses' station. But I can imagine how it got there."

"Okay, how?"

"Well it was a new prescription, right?"

"Uh-huh."

"So whoever was delivering meds ..."

"Jennifer?"

"No. Not a hospice nurse. A med tech delivering meds room to room. And she would, maybe, take a new bottle with her to check with the patient that she agreed with the prescription."

"That sounds like good procedure."

"Could be. Anyway, Zinnia probably received more than one pill. Staff has a lot of patients to see. She's got a pill trolley in the hall. Who knows what's on her mind. She's not paying close attention. The bottle gets left behind."

"That's a simple explanation of how it got in the room."

Willow examined her hands. "Yeah, it gets trickier after that."

"Right. That story - to that point - is business as usual."

"Zinnia discovers the bottle, sticks it in the drawer, she'll tell somebody about it later."

"Only that doesn't explain what happened to all the pills."

"No," Willow shook her head. "No it does not."

"So maybe Zinnia saw an opportunity to end her misery by taking the pills, the whole bottle and ..."

"Another possibility," said Willow, "is she didn't so much take advantage of the staff mistake ..."

"She deliberately hid the bottle from her."

Willow clenched her jaw then said, "Would Zinnia have done that?"

Lance shook his head. "Who knows? Who knows?"

They sat quietly then after a bit Lance got up to turn on lights. Willow turned and watched him for a moment or so. "Lance?" Her voice was soft, tentative.

"Yeah, hon, what is it?"

"Would you ...?" She considered his face.

"Would I what?"

"I don't know. I think I lost my train of thought."

Zinnia's Girls Memorial Service at the Ladies of Charity House

As the group murmured in response to Christy an Hispanic woman who couldn't have been eighteen years old began to speak from the front row.

"I'm not good at, you know, talking in front of, uh, people, and, uh, I wouldn't do this for, well anyone, no one, but for Miss Zinnia. Whew, I dunno ladies, I'm not - well, okay I'm gonna go ahead and do this," she said as she stood. "Oh yeah, I'm Serena. I love my little girl so much I gave her up to someone who will raise her right. When I started to show I had to hide from everybody I knew. I couldn't let anyone see me. Uh, well, you know what I'm saying. That's the great thing about bein' here. Nobody has to really explain much. But it is good, like some of you said, to tell your story. That's the great thing you Ladies have done for us. You give us a place to talk where you don't haveta look over your shoulder to see who's listening. So anyway Miss Zinnia told me I could let someone have my baby who would really love her and take good care and give her the things I never had. I never really saw my baby and no one told me 'You had a girl.' But I know she was. And I'm going to see her someday. Miss Zinnia and me and my baby - we'll get together and baby girl and me will thank Miss Zinnia 'cause she found such a good home for my baby. I, uh, well, that's all." Serena fell back into her chair.

Chapter Seventeen

At the dining table everyone seemed to be in a private fog, working out personal issues of one sort or another. Willow surfaced from her deep thoughts to question whether television might offer anything for the family. She received a variety of grunts and mutterings. Gayle pushed her plate away from her and then pulled it back. Then she leaned over it and began turning the plate in a circle. Willow watched her for a minute and then leaned forward looking into Gayle's eyes.

"What's up Missy? Looks like you haven't actually eaten a bite."

"I ate a little."

Lance rejoined the family from his mental rehearsal of a sermon and checked out Gayle's array of food. "Very little," he noted.

"Well, I've been too busy thinking."

"Apparently we all have," muttered Zach.

"So," said Willow, "what about?"

"Ah, stuff," Gayle said.

"Like?" asked her dad.

"Friends ... and all the things bothering them."

Zach said, "Hmmpf," and grabbed a bun from the bread basket.

Lance nodded. "You both have been worried about your friends quite a bit."

"We're proud of both of you," said Willow.

"Well, I know you think it's important to help people when they have needs or problems."

"Uh-huh," answered Lance as he gave his wife a questioning glance. "Has your friend come up with a solution?"

"Not really." Gayle pushed her empty plate aside.

"Have you come up with something you want to suggest to her?"

"Umm - well first, I don't believe I have told you yet who it is."

Lance stroked his chin. "The only thing you have said for certain is that you're not the one pregnant."

Zach laughed and slapped the table. "That's clear enough."

Willow frowned at Zach but he continued to laugh.

Gayle braced her arms on the table leaning toward her brother. "What? You don't think anybody wants to get me pregnant?"

Zach stopped laughing and just looked at Gayle. Both parents also stared open-mouthed at their daughter.

Suddenly Gayle sat back and looked from one parent to the other.

"I didn't mean," she started and then waved a hand at Zach. "I was just saying ... I mean. I'm not ..."

"Okay," said Lance, "we know, we know. And Zach knows you're attractive enough just not interested."

Willow folded her arms across her chest. "I don't think I would have said it quite like that."

"Whatever, but I think we have interrupted something Gayle wanted to talk about."

With that three of the Carrolls turned expectantly toward Gayle.

"Oh," she put her hand to her mouth. "Right. Uh, first I was about to tell you that Nancy is the one who is pregnant."

"You're kidding," said Zach. "I didn't know that."

"Ah," said Willow. "I guessed it would be her or Rosita."

"Yes, it's Nancy. And I'm pretty sure this is going to be a disaster in her family."

"She hasn't told them yet?" said Lance.

"She hasn't told anyone but me and Rosita."

"Has she seen a doctor?" asked her mother.

"No. She hasn't seen a doctor, hasn't told her parents, hasn't told the boy."

"Who's the guy?" asked Zach.

"Don't know. She won't tell us."

Lance pushed his chair back and crossed his legs. "Has she made any decision about the baby?"

"She can't, Dad. She needs an accepting environment and more heads, hearts, and arms around her than just Rosita and me."

"Oh," said Lance and Willow together.

"Oh what?" asked Zach.

Ignoring her brother Gayle said, "Yeah, I want Nancy to move in with us."

Lucinda watched Lance enter the lobby. Catching his eye she waved him toward her.

"What's up?" he said.

"Miss Zinnia has company."

"Oh?" he raised his shoulders. "Who would that be?"

"Her brother from back East."

"Ah ha, some family finally showed up."

The door to Zinnia's room stood partially open and Lance could see the back of a slender man about his size. At the sound of his knock, the man turned. Zinnia appeared to be asleep. The man stepped out of the room, closing the door behind him. Lance introduced himself as Zinnia's pastor.

"Glad to meet you," he said. "Zinnie has mentioned you. I'm her brother Xavier."

"Zinnie, is it?"

The brother chuckled. "Only Yosef and I call her that."

"Xavier, Yosef and Zinnia?"

"Yes, except it's the other way around - Z, Y, and X. Zinnia's the eldest, I'm youngest. Our parents had a weird sense of humor. They never explained themselves."

"Are you the scientist or the pharmacist?"

Xavier half stepped back. "Why, I'm both. A pharmacist is a scientist." He smiled to show he wasn't really offended. "I'm just not the astrophysicist."

Lance pointed at the door behind Xavier's back. "How's she doing?"

The brother shook his head. "Could we sit somewhere?"

Lance nodded and led the way to the cafeteria.

Xavier retrieved a cup of coffee for himself and a soft drink for Lance from a vending machine. They seated themselves at a corner table.

"I knew before I got here she had stage four cancer but," he shook his head. "I don't know. It's just a shock." He searched his coffee cup for solace.

Lance waited a moment to respect the emotion in Xavier's statement.

"Will your brother be coming?"

"No. He's in Europe doing a lecture tour. Last time we talked we both thought there was plenty of time for him to finish the tour and ..." He looked over Lance's shoulder. "He can't possibly be here for another six weeks. And that ..." He sighed.

"Any other family available to come?"

"Hmmpf!" - something of a sarcastic laugh.

"I'm afraid I'm it. None of us quite see eye-to-eye with Zinnia. Sef and I flew off to the Northeast but we and our wives are all true Kansas Republicans. Zinnie never really could be that conservative. I guess I'm the closest to her way of thinking." He thought about that for a moment. "I'm not really that close."

"But," Lance raised his hands. "You're still family."

"Yes," he drew it out. "But there are issues." Xavier rearranged himself and pointed at Lance, indicating a story to be unfolded. "We learned earlier in Zinnie's teaching career that she was providing extracurricular help to her students. Well, at first we couldn't help be proud of what she was doing. We encouraged it. Sef even sent her some money. Then we learned some of the female students might have gotten abortions. We don't believe in that."

"Oh." Lance leaned back and gave a quick nod.

"Yeah. That put a chill on the relationship."

"Well, still ..."

Xavier raised a hand. "It got worse."

Lance shook his head.

"Sef's wife wrote a very strongly worded letter. Sef told me some of what she said. I told him I hoped Zinnia opened it with asbestos gloves. We had little contact after that. And then she quit teaching and started this counseling service. We got a short note about that. Sort of took it as business as usual for her. None of us responded to her note, but then we got a formal brochure from one of her co-founders describing the service and asking for contributions. My wife called Sef's wife and the two of them went ballistic. Nobody wrote a fiery letter but ..." Xavier shook his head. "I guess we unofficially wrote Zinnia out of the family."

Lance didn't know what to say.

Xavier drank a sip of coffee.

"I read the brochure. It really sounds like a creative activity. Abortion is presented as the tail-end, last resort option. I never argued the case. I mean do you side with your wife who lives with you here in Baltimore or with your sister way out there in Albuquerque?" He raised his hands. "No contest."

Xavier seemed to have finished his story and Lance still could think of nothing to say. Finally he asked, "How long will you be here?"

"Now that I'm here I feel like the right thing to do is to stay a while - maybe until, well ... But I can't. I'm flying back home tomorrow."

Frank waddled out from under the dining table and starred at Lance. The silence in the room was so intense he sensed something must be out of place.

"Is her home situation that bad?" asked Willow.

Gayle sighed. "They have problems like you wouldn't believe. I mean her dad is pretty much crippled up and can't earn enough and her mom asked her to quit school and get a job. And she probably will have to do that anyway - quit school at least."

"Is this something you and Nancy have discussed," wondered Lance, "or just your idea?"

Gayle fidgeted a bit and leaned over to pick up Frank. "Yeah, well, we sorta talked about it in kinda general terms. I, uh, didn't want to go too far, get her hopes up until we had ... I wanted your okay before I said too much."

Willow leaned forward to look directly at Gayle. "What exactly did you have in mind, Gayle? Did you plan for her to stay here until the baby is born, or longer?"

Gayle continued to focus her attention on Frank. "Oh, not longer. But I imagine she'll have to get a job and an apartment."

Lance said, "She's decided to keep the baby."

"Yes." At that Gayle let Frank jump back down to the floor. Gayle looked up at her father. "That turns out to be the least unacceptable choice."

"You know about the Ladies of Charity, the organization Zinnia Foster started. They do wonderful work with pregnant teenagers."

"But they basically just help girls arrange adoptions or abortions, don't they?"

Lance's eyebrows raised. Willow reached for Gayle's hand.

"No hon," said Lance. "They do a lot more. Their chief service is simply to supply compassionate company for the pregnant girl. Something along the lines of what you and Rosita are doing for Nancy, but with more experience. They often find a girl a place to live during her pregnancy, if that is needed. Why do you think Nancy needs to move out of her home?"

"Well, like I was saying, it's just going to get too hard. Her parents are going to push her to help support them. If she weren't living there maybe her mom and dad could handle just taking care of themselves all right. Besides by not being in the house with them she wouldn't have to deal with their judgmentalism."

"Running away," said Willow.

"I suppose."

"I'm not opposed to her moving in with us for a short time," said Lance, "but let's try to learn what help she really needs and then what would be required to get her that help."

"I think she just needs a place to stay."

"Uh-huh," said Willow. "She needs that. She needs medical care and a plan for paying for that. She needs counseling to help her decide how she's going to provide basic food, shelter and clothing for herself and her baby. If we agree on her living here, where would she sleep and what part of your chores would she take on as her responsibility?"

"I didn't think any of that would be a problem. She's a responsible girl. She'd carry her load."

"Right," said Lance rather matter-of-factly. "Why don't you see if she will go with the two of us to the Ladies of Charity House and get her introduced to some people who understand all of this better than we do."

Lance assumed he would never see Conrad Johansson or Wanda Braun, the couple he had counselled in San Marcos in the first two weeks of his ministry, again. He was wrong about that, too. About Conrad anyway. He had grown in his pastorate and a few people had begun to spread the word that here was a young preacher who had valuable insights to share. He had proved himself smart enough to capture the heart of a local girl and he and his wife were considering a career move to a church in the eastern part of the state, a place that also seemed to have nursing opportunities for Willow.

Lance struggled with the emotions of a letter of resignation to be delivered to a congregation he had learned to love when a shadow fell across his desk.

"Pastor Lance, you may not remember me."

When Lance looked up at the haunted blue eyes under a blond crew-cut, he knew exactly who stood before his desk.

Lance led Conrad out back to a picnic table under a pecan tree and told him how glad he was to see him.

"Is Wanda still part of your life?"

"No, not really. Well, she was. We did get married. But I wasn't worth staying with."

"I'm sure that's not true. What happened?"

"Yeah, well, what happened - that's why I came by. I mean, I see a counselor regularly but I just wanted to spend a few minutes with you."

"Really? Why is that?"

"For one thing, to say thanks."

"I can't imagine what for. I never felt I was much help to you."

"I s'pose I can understand that. We pretty much had our minds made up. We didn't come to you to tell us what to do. I guess you saw that and - I dunno - you probably were frustrated by us."

"Why did you come to me?"

"We didn't even know at the time. Someone said you seemed like a nice guy. We were looking for a nice guy."

"Uh ..."

"We needed someone to listen to us and not judge. We were pretty sure what we

245

were going to do but we wanted to say it out loud in front of somebody else and see what it sounded like. We couldn't find that somebody until, well, we heard you were nice."

"Stellar recommendation."

"Worked for us. We needed someone to hear us without hating us."

"Yeah, I guess I did that."

"Yes, you did."

"So, is that your problem now? Is someone hating you?"

"No, no way. If anything people think I'm a hero because I served in the Gulf War."

"Ah. Well, good. Thanks for your service."

They sat quietly for a moment. Lance watched Conrad who was hunched over. He seemed to be processing what he would say next.

"So, nobody hates you."

"Just me."

"Just you. What's that about?"

"Pastor Lance, I killed people, shot 'em."

"Under orders. Kill or be killed. You say you're seeing a counselor. PTSD?"

"Yes. That's what it's called."

"And that got between you and Wanda?"

"Oh did it ever. I'd say she still loves me and I love her, but she can't live with me. I can't allow her to live with me. Neither one of us can trust me."

"Conrad, it was war. Someone had to do what you did. You're allowed."

"That doesn't make it right."

"Maybe not. This is above my pay-grade, beyond my training. Fortunately you're getting professional help better than I can give. But I can listen. Since we last talked I've learned a little more about listening."

Conrad stood, signaling he was about to leave.

"I just needed to be reminded that somewhere there's a nice guy in this world. That helps."

Zinnia's Girls Memorial Service at the Ladies of Charity House

Dorcus had met Lance at the door and had taken charge of arrangements. She was one of the clients but it seemed the Ladies who actually ran the program let Dorcus exercise a great deal of leadership. She now stood and cleared her throat.

"People call me Big Sis but my name is Dorcus. Almost no one knows that 'cause everyone knows me as Big Sis but when I turned up pregnant I needed a bigger sister. I was so ashamed of myself. Alicia over there, she told me about the Ladies and that's when I met Miss Zinnia. Alicia had to almost twist my arm to get me to show up here. I don't know if you can - well, of course you know. One thing I've learned - we all learned it - I'm not the only one. But I thought I was. You see I'm always the one in charge. I'm just the leader of the pack. Everything always works out the way I want it to be. And then I got pregnant. I didn't want to be pregnant. It couldn't happen to me but it did. Miss Zinnia told me, 'You can take charge of this. You can get back on top. But first you gotta ask for help.' And she made me say that. She said to me, 'Tell me you want my help.' I just looked at her but she insisted. I bowed my head and cried. I don't cry. No one can make me cry. But I did. Oh, well look at me now. Thank you Miss Penny. I should have brought some tissue but I never need it. So anyway, I thought that was the lowest point of my whole life. I actually said, 'Please. I need help.' And you know what she said? Well probably you do know because she said a lot of the same things to all of us. But what she said was, 'Do you know how much strength it takes to ask for help?' I didn't see that as being strong but I guess she was right. So, you see what I'm saying? I needed a big sister so I could return to being the Big Sis. I love volunteering here. Like a lot of you guys my contract with the Ladies says I come back and play big sister to the next girls that come in here. I have to say to Miss Zinnia, Thank you. Because of you I got my mojo back."

Chapter Eighteen

On Saturday the Carrolls were in a hurry to get to the Balloon Fiesta field to help launch Lindsey Davis' balloon. But no matter they had started out at 5:30 in the A of the M, the traffic snail-scooted toward the field. The two week-ends of the fiesta always produced huge crowds. When they finally snaked through close to the park, they were able to branch off into the balloon crew parking area - a perk gained from attaching themselves to the Davis team. Anticipating riding in the chase vehicle to help secure the balloon when it landed and load it into Davis' specially designed trailer, the Carroll family rushed toward the field through rows of vendor kiosks heading for the Davis' assigned launch pad. The whole process was more fun than work. Lindsey and his wife June took care of the skilled responsibilities required for inflating the balloon. The Carrolls helped lay out the balloon after having sent Zach and Gayle to buy them breakfast burritos at one of the kiosks. Lindsey and June set up the fan that started the inflation process and then ignited the burner used to complete the inflation and eventually fly the balloon.

None of the four Carrolls could be pulled away from watching the balloon come to life. Originally it was nothing more than a large, multi-colored ground cover. But then it began to take shape and rise up. In fits and starts it rose over them and finally began to strain against the restraining lines. It was time to fly. Gently the balloon and basket separated from the ground. A rhythm of whooshes pushed the balloon higher and then it was time to play chase crew.

June drove the van pulling the trailer. The Carrolls rode with her. Lindsey and June communicated by way of a small radio.

"How do you know which way to drive?" asked Zach.

"Well this appears to be an ordinary ballooning day so I'll just head for your house," June said. "Maybe Lindsey will land in your backyard.

"Really," said a bug-eyed Gayle.

"Probably not. Ballooning's not that precise. But, if he wanted to, he could get close. However, that's not what he wants to do today. You saw the two guys who are paying for this ride. Lindsey will try to set down in a convenient place for us to load the balloon in our trailer and get all of us back to the park in time to take a second group up."

Suddenly June's radio crackled to life.

"Hey there June-bug." The Carrolls recognized Lindsey's voice.

"What's up, old man," June responded.

"From the looks of the leaders it appears we'll end up close to CNM West Side."

"Gotcha."

June explained that considering the wind directions it appeared the balloons would fly a typical Albuquerque box. That meant Lindsey would either rise or drop to find an altitude where the wind would change directions. By managing his altitude Lindsey could fly north at a low altitude and then fire up his burner, gain altitude, find a wind change taking the balloon south and end up not too far from where he started. Lindsey kept his wife informed when they changed directions. Occasionally one or another Carroll would catch sight of the Davis balloon but not often. Sometimes the terrain would hide it or other balloons would shield it from view. June, for her part, simply concentrated on driving to where she expected Lindsey to land. At the end of the trip - that is for the balloon and for the chase vehicle - they met in a desolate patch on a hill in the west mesa of Albuquerque. The support crew (the Carrolls) rushed to grab lines and secure the balloon, helped roll it up and stash the basket, the burner and the balloon where Lindsey or June pointed. The Davises and the paying riders held a brief celebration and then all piled into the van for the return to the balloon park.

The whole experience duplicated itself except this time the riders were a mother and her teen-age daughter. Zach hadn't met the girl before but he certainly paid close attention to her. The second trip went a slightly different route. This time the balloon landed in a middle school soccer field.

"Great job," smiled Lindsey after a successful return to the Balloon Fiesta Park. "Now we plan your ascension."

Zach and Gayle thought the day for their balloon ride would never come. But come it did. Again they rushed to the balloon park but this time they would be riding. They had dressed warmly as Lindsey had instructed them to do. "You know it'll be cool on the ground but wait'll we get some altitude."

Once again the Carrolls enjoyed watching the magic of the balloon taking life.

Zach, Gayle, Willow, and Lance filed into the basket with Lindsey. The gas burner whooshed to fill the balloon with hot air. Lance and Zach watched the fire as if they could see some magical power forcing the balloon to rise.

"Wow," said Gayle, "we're off the ground!"

"What," said Zach. "I didn't feel a thing."

"That's amazing," said Willow. "You can't tell you're going up."

Lindsey laughed. "Everyone expects an experience like an elevator lifting but you don't feel a thing. And, except for my little furnace here, you won't hear anything either."

"Oh, look at the Rio Grande," said Gayle.

Lindsey offered them a splash and dash and to their surprise the balloon began to drop toward the river. Just at the point where the basket touched the water the Carrolls heard the whoosh. Heated air lifted the balloon back into the sky.

For the next three-quarters of an hour the Carrolls oohed, aahed, and pointed. Much of

Albuquerque or Rio Rancho they recognized. Some scenes confused them but when Lindsey explained what they were seeing, they would exclaim how different it looked when looking down on it.

Lance pointed at three balloons that had companioned them through the ride.

"Boy they're rising fast," he said

"No," Lindsey said, "we're dropping like a rock."

"Huh?"

Sure enough, when they looked at the ground, it was climbing to meet them.

Lance nodded as Lindsey explained, "Happens a lot. You think you see another balloon on the rise when you're really dropping."

"Same with people's lives," said Lance.

"Yep," said Zach, "in the toilet."

"We're about to land," Lindsey instructed. "Flex your knees and relax. You'll feel a little bump."

Willow snickered. "Is that like when the nurse says you'll feel a little stick?"

"Well, no. The nurse is lying to you."

On the way home the Carrolls agreed this had been one of the best experiences they had shared.

"There she is, Dad." Gayle pointed at Nancy who sat at the picnic table under a domed covering, her back toward them. Gayle had convinced Nancy that she should talk with Lance about her predicament and Nancy had reluctantly agreed to meet them at a city park in the north part of Rio Rancho. Gayle and Lance quickly seated themselves, Gayle beside Nancy and Lance across from the girls.

Gayle gave Nancy a quick squeeze. "How ya doing, girlfriend."

"Okay," Nancy spoke quietly. "Hello, Mr. Carroll."

Lance smiled at her. "Hi, Nancy. You look like you're doing well."

"I'm not, no matter how I look." She ducked her head and then looked up at Lance. "Mr. Carroll, am I just truly an awful person?"

"Certainly not," he said forcefully. "You are just truly a distressed person and we're here to see if we can help you with that."

"I don't see how anyone can help me."

"Of course you don't. That's why it's so good that you've let some friends into your secret."

"Yeah, well, I'm about to the point where it's not going to be much of a secret." She let a brief laugh escape.

"How much of a secret is it now?"

"How do you mean?"

"Well for one thing, do your parents know?"

Tears leaked down Nancy's cheek. She hiccupped a weak "No."

"Would you mind if I made a couple of suggestions?"

"I guess I really need all the help I can get."

Lance opened his mouth to respond but Nancy continued, "I don't really want to ask for help but I'm beginning to realize I don't have much choice. I don't feel like I have any choices. This is so bad and it's about to get awfully, terribly worse."

"No. It's not all bad and it's about to get maybe minimally, marginally better."

"Better?"

"Sure. You can make it better by doing two things. I'm going to suggest just two things for you to do. You can handle two things, can't you?"

"I guess."

"One's hard and the other is easy. First the hard. It's hard but you can do it. Get the hard done and right away everything begins to be better - a little better." Lance paused and saw that he had Nancy's anxious, serious attention. "Tell your parents."

Nancy looked paralyzed but she nodded her head almost unperceptively.

"Gayle will go with you or I'll go with you or Gayle and I or Gayle and Rosita. You can do it alone if you prefer, but get it done."

"Yes sir."

"Second is an easy thing. I'd like to introduce you to the Ladies of Charity House. They have a lot of experience helping girls who have found themselves in exactly the same situation where you are now. You can see what that's like. If they have something that appeals to you, great. If you don't like it, walk away. No harm done. Okay."

"Can I think about it?"

Lance nodded and sat for a moment.

"Nancy," he said, leaning toward her, "I don't want you to feel any pressure from me."

She nodded and tears leaked down her cheeks.

"Sure, you can think about it. It will not hurt my feelings in the least if you choose not to follow my suggestions. I'm just trying to help. But you already said your secret's about to reveal itself."

The sun dropped toward Mount Taylor. Lance offered Nancy a ride home which she accepted. On the way to Nancy's no one said a word. After depositing her at her front door. Gayle turned to her father with a broad smile. "Thanks, Dad."

"Well, that's a minimal start, Sis. We've got a long way to go."

"I know, but you said, 'We.' That lightens the load."

Zinnia's Girls Memorial Service at the Ladies of Charity House

The silence in the room as "Big Sis" returned to her chair told me the respect the other girls had for her. It took a minute or so before another woman spoke.

"That was so good. All of you. Hi I'm Suzanna. Today I'm getting one of the things I got here when I was pregnant. I'm hearing you tell your stories and I'm remembering I'm not the only one. All of our stories have happy endings. I know not everyone agrees with me but let me put it this way. What is your story without Miss Zinnia? See! When you came to the Ladies for help your story took a happy ending turn - or at least a better ending than it would have been otherwise. When I was about eight months gone I was miserable. I was heavy. I was hot. I was big, huge. Can you imagine? I came in here one day wearing a red tent. I swear, it was twenty yards of red material that my mama had sewn together to cover me up. It was a dark cloudy day and that window over there became a mirror. By the way, you ever notice there are no mirrors in this place? What's that all about? Black clouds turned that window into a mirror and I saw this freak standing there looking like a gigantic tomato. You know, like you're traveling Route 66 and there's a sign that says 'Come see the world's biggest tomato!' And that would be me. Yeah. When I saw that I just busted out crying. Miss Zinnia came running in to see what was going on. 'I'm a giant tomato!' I said that. I was wailing. 'I'm a giant tomato.' She hugged me. She was a hugger wasn't she? Look at all your heads nod. Then she backed off and looked me up and down and shook her head. She said, 'An apple is more like it.' And, for a minute I thought maybe she's trying to hurt my feelings. She turned to look at me in the window and she says, 'A beach ball is better yet.' Then she pointed at her image in the window. She was wearing that green smock she often had on and she said, 'Now there's a green bean.' And I started laughing and I said, 'Green chili pepper is more like it.' She said, 'wouldn't we look good on a Christmas tree.' I just laughed and laughed. Yeah we all cried here, but didn't we have some good laughs?"

Albuquerque Journal
January 26, 2015
NM Appeals Court Hears Right to Die
Arguments
by Russell Contreras / Associated Press

Do terminally ill patients in New Mexico already have a right to end their lives?

That's what the New Mexico Court of Appeals is set to decide after hearing arguments Monday from the state and lawyers from a terminally ill woman.

Chapter Nineteen

Taking advantage of their break from school Zach and Gayle biked to the volcanoes. The Rio Grande rift represented a major geological shift of the earth's plates. One result was a river running from Colorado all through New Mexico and dividing Texas from Old Mexico. Another result was the five volcanic projections on the west side of Albuquerque. The Carroll siblings decided to prove their athletic capabilities by biking to and around at least one volcano.

On their return home they arrived at an intersection coincident with Deloit on his bike.

"Headed to work?" asked Zach.

"Oh yeah. Got to earn some money."

The three dismounted. The boys grabbed hands and shoulder hugged. Deloit and Gayle gave each other quick waves.

"So how many jobs are you working?" said Zach.

"Just two. How'd you know I had more than one?"

"Word circulates."

"Sir-cue-lates, right. Well I just said, got to earn some money."

"You going on an African safari or something. I don't know another dude that needs that much money."

"I do," he said and threw a leg over his bike.

"Whoa, wait a minute Deloit. Don't run off on me. I'm trying to be your friend here."

Deloit looked at Zach then Gayle. His frown suggested he wasn't buying Zach's claim of friendship but then he pulled his leg back and balanced himself against his bicycle.

"Really?"

Zach nodded.

Gayle spoke up. "Zach's been really concerned about you Deloit. He worries about you a lot."

Deloit appeared surprised. "Really?" This time his voice gave a different inflection to his question.

"Yeah," said Zach.

Deloit rubbed his forehead. "This is not a good story." He turned his back to the Carrolls and leaned on his bike. Slowly he turned around to face them again.

"You see my dad lost his job."

"I didn't know that," said Zach stunned.

Deloit nodded. "Yeah, and we don't have any money to fall back on."

Gayle said, "So you're working to keep the family afloat."

"Well sure but not at first. There's more to the story." Deloit pulled off his cap and rubbed his head. "See, he got desperate and got caught shoplifting a watch so he could buy us some groceries."

"Oh no," said Gayle.

"Yeah. He's in jail."

"Really?" said Zach. "For how long?"

"He should get out this week. It wasn't that big a deal. The judge took a pretty lenient direction. But it means he's got even less chance of finding a job now."

"That's terrible," said Gayle.

Her brother agreed. "Anything we can do?"

"Got an extra hundred or two dollars lying around?"

The three young people suddenly found they had run out of talk. Awkwardly they said good-bye and went their different directions.

"What a story," said Gayle.

Zach shook his head then looked up remembering something. "I thought you didn't think I was concerned enough about Deloit."

"You weren't."

"Well why did you tell him I was worried about him?"

"Because that's what he needed to hear. He needed encouragement, not the truth."

Lance put down the book he wasn't reading. Somehow he couldn't keep his mind on what was becoming a foggy explanation for why evil persisted in a world God had declared a good creation. He rewound a memory of a circular argument he had chased with Rabbi Benny.

Benny had asked, "Do you want to uncover the perpetrator or cover up the deed?"

Lance responded, "What would best protect the innocent?"

"The innocent?"

"Right. The perpetrator - to use your term - may have acted, but the act is innocent."

"Ah ha. I didn't realize your alter ego was Polly Anna."

"Oh give me a break. I'm being a realist here."

"Not an idealist?"

"No, not at all. If you prefer, let me put it this way: what does the least harm?"

"Okay. I'll take that. So, has any harm been done to this point?"

"No. I don't think so. A lovely person died but with less pain than would have been the case if she had lived another week or so."

"All right. The next question then would be, what future harm can be prevented?"

Lance remembered nodding his head vigorously. "A lot of harm could build up if malicious gossip is allowed to poison the reputations of good people."

"I talked to Nancy," Gayle announced as she sat at the table. "She told her parents."

"How'd that go," asked Willow.

"Not great, but like Dad told her, she got the hard part done. Her mom cried and her dad just sat there. Never said a word. The good part was that she told them she was going to the Ladies of Charity House and she had a plan and it would all be taken care of."

"What did her parents think about that?" said Lance.

"Like before, her mother cried and her dad just sat there."

"What's her plan?" asked Willow.

"To go see the Ladies with Dad and me."

"And?"

"And that's it. She doesn't really have anything else. She told me she just said that to cut down on her parents' questions and arguments."

Lance asked, "Did they have any questions or arguments?"

"Like I said ..."

"Mom cried, dad sat."

"You got it."

"Well, the hard part is out of the way."

"One of them, anyway."

Zinnia asked Lance to help her sit up a little better against her stack of pillows.

"Is that better?" he asked.

"Good enough," she said. Her voice was quieter but not as strong as in previous conversations with her pastor.

Lance sat and glanced around the room. "How're you doing?"

"Okay. My dad used to say, 'I'm in good shape for the shape I'm in.' Or something like that."

Lance smiled.

"Xavier gone already?"

"I'm surprised he even came at all."

"How'd the visit go?"

"He can be nice when he's away from Joe and their wives."

"Ah-ha, 'Joe' rather than 'Yosef'!"

"Yeah. After my dad died I decided to call him Joe. 'Xavier' and 'Zinnia' were all right but 'Yosef' was too pretentious. I called him 'Joe' and mom and Xavier settled on 'Sef' - both of which he accepted."

"So, not much attachment to your brothers or their families."

Zinnia shrugged and closed her eyes. After a bit she said, "Had an unexpected visitor."

"Oh. Who came by?"

"Big Sis." She watched Lance furrow his brow. "One of my girls. She had big problems and eventually became one of my best helpers. Sweet of her to come by. She's the only one to do so - and that's fine by me. I really see no need for them to see me like this."

"So you don't have visitors," a statement.

"Well my widows come around. But they need to quit. It's really hard for them."

"They're grieving for you."

"Yes. They will grieve for a bit."

"And you?"

"You don't miss much, do you, preacher?"

Lance smirked, crossed his ankles.

"I'm about through. Not that many tears, but some. I went through a huge grief when I lost Mr. Foster. That was a big loss for me."

"More so than your parents?"

Zinnia flipped a hand. "I was too young to understand what happened to my dad. Mom lived a pretty full life and I was sorry to see her go." She looked toward the curtained window. "Yeah, I grieved some but I was happy for her to be released."

The two friends settled into the quiet for a moment.

"I've grieved," Zinnia continued. "It's not easy leaving this life, but I'm ready." She paused. "I'm sorry to be leaving my girls and some friends, but I'm about done with the grief. Certainly ready to be done with the pain."

Lance nodded. "What are you expecting?"

"No idea."

He raised his eyebrows.

"Sure, I've thought about what comes next. But I don't know and don't believe anybody else knows."

"What about those near death stories you read about?"

"I suppose they're comforting for the ones who experience them. But nobody really knows what they mean. Are they a foretaste of heaven or just some expanded dream state?" She looked at Lance. "I'm not arguing either way. It's just - well, far as we know only One has crossed over and come back to tell about it."

She winced and closed her eyes.

Lance sat forward. "Too much?"

She nodded.

After a moment Zinnia whispered, "Help me scoot down and then please go away."

He did as she asked.

Zinnia's Girls Memorial Service at the Ladies of Charity House

As everyone laughed a dark complexioned young woman walked to the front of the room carrying something wrapped in brown paper.

"Hi. I'm Tamara and that's my baby girl back there, Maria. You've all made hard choices because of Miss Zinnia's help. My choice wasn't any harder than yours but it sure was not easy. In my pueblo getting pregnant is a responsibility to the people. But getting pregnant by a white boy you're not married to is a violation of that responsibility. Luckily I found the Ladies House and Miss Zinnia helped me think about what choices I had. I told her one day I had betrayed the responsibility I had for my people; so she asked me to find a new responsibility and I did. I would have married him but he would not go for it. So what was my responsible choice? For me it was being a mother to Maria. Now that's not an easy trail to walk. I have had to face up to my actions. Fortunately Miss Zinnia put me in touch with an art gallery in Old Town. I paint. And I do some good stuff even if it's me saying so. So Maria and me, we manage. I brought something today. Miss Penny, Miss Betsy, Miss Victoria I want to give this to the Ladies House. Suzanna if you'll help me get this unwrapped." Suzanna stepped forward as requested and the two of them peeled away paper to reveal a remarkable likeness of Zinnia Foster. "Oh, you like it. I'm so glad. This is my memory of Miss Zinnia at her desk. That smile just says, 'I'm so glad to see you.'"

Chapter Twenty

Mid-morning on a crisp autumn day revealed Lance holding the door for Nancy and Gayle to enter the Ladies of Charity House. A young, dark skinned woman with long, glossy black hair tied in a ponytail greeted them and introduced herself as Beatrice. She looked to be at least eight-months pregnant. Beatrice led them to an interview room where the girls met Victoria.

"Oh Lance," Victoria said, "I'm so happy to get to meet your daughter. Gayle you have a wonderful father."

"He thinks so," Gayle laughed. "And so do I."

"Nancy, it's nice to meet you, too. Everyone have a seat."

The room was furnished with comfortable captain's chairs. A Georgia O'Keeffe floral print hung on one wall. The East wall featured a large window looking at the Sandias. Opposite the window was a rustic painting of a New Mexico landscape which might have also been by O'Keeffe. The feel of the room was welcoming.

Nancy had entered nervous, almost to the point of nausea, but Victoria's smile and the feel of the room encouraged her to relax.

"What would you like for us to do for you, Nancy?"

Nancy looked at Lance and Gayle, then back to Victoria. "I, uh, I don't really know."

Victoria's smile charmed them all. "That's often the case, though sometimes girls come in with a list of requests. Either way, we try to help. I have some questions and some suggestions. You should know, and meeting Beatrice as you came in helps make this clear, you are not alone."

Nancy looked back at the door as if searching for Beatrice. "Is she, I mean will she," Nancy turned back to Victoria. "Uh, will she keep her baby or uh ..."

Victoria smiled and shrugged. "You'd have to ask Beatrice. If she wants to share that information, and some girls do, others don't, she will. Beatrice is pretty open. You would have that same privacy. Everyone here respects your decisions."

"Oh, of course. I didn't mean ..."

"Sure, no problem. I understand." Victoria waved her hand indicating Gayle and Lance. "You have a pretty impressive support group here. How do you know these people? Do you attend Reverend Carroll's church?"

"Uh, no, not his church. Well, really, I don't go anywhere. Well I might. I haven't thought about that. I just ..."

"It's okay Nancy. I'm not trying to put you on the spot. I'm just impressed with the company you keep."

"Oh yeah. Gayle's my best friend. Well, one of my two best friends." Nancy looked at Gayle. "You know, we could have asked Rosita to come with us."

Gayle laughed and then covered her mouth. "Excuse me," she said toward Victoria. "I was just a little surprised." Turning back to Nancy, "We talked about it and you changed your mind three or four times."

"Yeah. I remember. And now I changed my mind again, but a little late."

Victoria turned on her charming smile and said, "Changing your mind is completely acceptable. On most things that is. There will come a time on a decision or two where you have to stick with a decision, but we can give you a lot of help with making choices you will be able to live with."

"Yeah. I'm beginning to understand what that means. It was really hard for me to decide to come here but Gayle - oh and Mr. Carroll, too - was so encouraging. I've been so afraid I was all alone with this and it's good to know that's not true."

After a few more questions Victoria told Nancy she could choose how much and what kind of help she wanted to receive, of course including the option of not any help at all. Nancy responded her most immediate concern was her schooling and so Victoria sketched a plan for tutoring that would lead toward her GED.

Lance rushed into Zinnia's room and found her in bed covered to her chin.

"Tell me what's happening."

Tears filled her eyes as she pulled the sheet over her mouth.

Lance knelt by the bed taking one of her hands in his.

"Somebody called you," she whispered.

"Yes, the receptionist said you asked her to call me."

"Uh-huh. ... Thanks."

"Sure. What's up?"

"I got frightened."

"You have reasons. You're allowed."

She looked away from him. "I don't understand."

Lance shifted to one knee but kept her hand in his.

"What is it? What don't you understand?"

She looked back at him.

"I'm not afraid of dying. I want to end this."

"Okay."

"And just out of the blue I got terribly scared."

"What scared you? What triggered this?"

She considered the question then nodded her head.

"Oh, right. I know."

"So tell me."

She pushed the covers back some. Lance sat on the floor with his knees under his chin.

"The woman across the hall screamed. I was napping. I do that a lot. I woke up, startled awake. I had forgotten what woke me. Now I remember. I just thought something awful had happened ... was happening ... was about to happen."

She nodded her head.

The two were silent for a while. Then Lance took both her hands in both of his and prayed.

"Lord, restore peace in precious Zinnia."

He sat on the floor holding her hand until she went to sleep.

"Hey Clem!"

Lance leaned over the 'gossip break' in the backyard fence yelling for Clem to come out and visit. In no time his efforts proved successful. Clem had apparently gotten to his backdoor quickly but once outside he ambled across the yard.

"S'up bro?"

"I need someone to stand under my tree and catch large heavy limbs."

"No way, man! No way. I thought I told you someone who could cut down that menace."

Lance laughed. "You did. I called him and he came out to see what it was I wanted done."

"And?"

"He's going to come later in the week and take it out."

"Good. You know I have lots of those little tree shoots on this side of my backyard. I won't be sorry to see it gone."

"No, we will definitely not miss the mess it creates. But you want to know what's interesting about that tree?"

"I dunno. Do I?"

"Sure. That's the reason I called you out here."

"Okay. So tell me."

"That tree is contraband. It's illegal in New Mexico."

"What? Did it stick up a bank? How can a tree become a criminal?"

"By taking over both our yards, I guess. Anyway you're not supposed to grow one of those stink trees in this state."

"Well I'll be." Clem scratched his head.

Lance nodded. "Everywhere I turn things are not what you think they are."

Zinnia's Girls Memorial Service at the Ladies of Charity House

The room buzzed in appreciation of the painting. The next speaker had to start twice to get attention. But the respect of this growing community quickly came.

"Me llamo Elena. I grew up with brothers but you, Big Sis, and the rest of you are my sisters now because of Senora Zinnia. I needed you when I was pregnant and we need each other now that Senora Zinnia has passed. Did you know she was never pregnant? Not many people know that, at least not many of us. She would tell you she had hundreds of children. Anybody who sat in her classes or who came through the House here was one of her children. She understood each of us so well that, I guess, you assumed she knew what it was like to be pregnant; but she never was. Reason I know: she said so. I was in her office - Tamara that picture is so great; that is Senora Zinnia. I was moaning about being pregnant. Yeah, sound familiar? And finally she says, 'Well I know it isn't all roses but, to be honest I kind of envy you.' 'Envy me?' I says. 'How come you envy me?' 'You've got a new life there inside you. I never felt that.' It was sort of a different moment with Senora Zinnia. In one way it was different but in another way it was not. It was the same in that you always knew she was right there with you. That's what I felt that day. Senora Zinnia was a close friend. One of my closest."

Chapter Twenty-one

The refrigerator just presented its offerings with no intelligent suggestions and for some reason Lance couldn't make his brain decide on what he wanted to drink. Finally he pulled a cranberry juice drink from the bottom shelf. Before he straightened up Willow's voice accused him: "How long are you going to hold that door open. I swear sometimes you're my worst teen-ager."

He spun around, grabbed her in a bear hug (causing her to drop a notebook and pen) and kissed her.

Pushing her away he asked, "What did you say vixen-lady?"

Robotic-like she chanted, "My mind is blank. The last thing I can remember is your vow to love, honor and obey me."

"Uh-oh, I must have short-circuited a synapse in your brain."

Lance set his drink on the counter so he could retrieve the notebook to hand it back to Willow.

"You dropped your handkerchief."

"A true gentleman would bring my to-do list up-to-date and promise to take over my chores."

"So the truth comes out. I'm a rogue."

Willow tossed her head, grabbed her notebook and found her pen under the kitchen table. After that she poured herself a cup of coffee and sat down with Lance in their den.

"You know, Lance, this has been a tough week for me."

"I'm very aware of that, hon."

"I've done a lot of thinking about the work we do caring for dying people. We really have an uphill battle making the point that there comes a time when the best you can do is to stop attempting to cure a disease and turn your attention to caring for the person."

"Can't you do both?"

"Of course. Most of the time. ... Not always."

They took a moment to reflect on what Willow had said. Then she started up again. "Assisting a suicide is a legal expression. To do that is to break the law. No business or profession can survive by breaking the law. We can't do that. We wouldn't do that. Jennifer never did that."

Lance sighed as he settled into his recliner.

"But you know," she continued, "being a companion through a life transition comes with friendship. Love compels it."

"You're calling death a life transition?"

"Well isn't it?"

"Yeah, I guess that's one way to put it," Lance mused.

Willow nodded as if agreeing with herself.

Lance took up the thread of Willow's comment. "You favor holding your friend's hand as she dies. But you can't allow anyone to think you aggressively helped ease her pain by facilitating her death."

"Don't make assisted suicide sound so benevolent and mannerly."

"It's not benevolent?"

"Maybe. But I can't think that way."

"I understand your point, Will, you're protecting your job and your friend."

"Absolutely!"

"Okay, let's drop the subject."

"I'm fine with that. ... Unless I need to vent some more."

"Hmmm. The rule has been amended to: You may say whatever you want or need to say; I will not say another word about it.

285

"Oh," he said, raising a hand, "did I tell you about the veterinarian I met when I went to the Vigils?"

"No, I never heard anything about that. You went to be with them when they had their dog put down."

"I did. And the vet who came to their home ..."

"I didn't know vets euthanized by home visits."

"They do. I didn't know that either, but they do - at least this one did."

"What about it?"

"He climbed all over my backside because I'm a preacher and preachers are no practical help when people are making end-of-life decisions about their loved ones."

"Talking about pets? But you were there with Norm and Cecilia."

"And he called that a contradiction. No, he wasn't talking about pets. He said I had the right idea about the Vigils' dog but we preacher types were on the wrong page when it came to people. Actually he had a bad experience with a family member who faced a painful death. I tried to explain it was a complicated ethical issue and ministers could be very much in tune with the complexities but he waved me off as irrelevant."

"And one thing about you preacher types, if you are not going to say another word about it, you are within four paragraphs of your conclusion."

The next day after Zinnia's panic attack Lance stopped by to see her. He found her sitting in her rocker.

"Any better?" he asked.

She smiled at him and then winced.

"Oops. What happened?"

"Just one of those pains that I don't want you to know is happening."

"Can't keep secrets from me."

She pointed at the other chair. "Sit."

And he did.

"I had a dream."

"Tell me."

"Three people appeared to me. Well, maybe they didn't appear. I'm not sure what I saw but I felt Mr. Foster with me. I don't think either one of us spoke. I just felt him. And then I knew my mother was there. Again we didn't speak and I can't say what I saw. But I learned something."

"Oh?"

"Yes. I know the answer to that question you asked me."

"What question?"

"You asked if I was expecting anything. I know what to expect."

"And that is ..."

"Peace. Yesterday you prayed for me to have peace. I have it. That's what heaven brings us, peace."

Lance pointed at her. "Ah ha. I like that."

He nodded his head several times and then stopped.

"Didn't you say there was a third person in your dream?"

"That's what I like about you. You pay attention."

"I try."

"Yes, there was a third person in my dream."

"Really. I'm not going to guess, so you will have to tell me."

She beamed a smile, this time without wincing.

Zinnia's Girls Memorial Service at the Ladies of Charity House

The women in the room had obviously gotten comfortable with one another. The next speaker anyone would have thought was too shy ordinarily to tell her story, but not on this occasion.

"You all know me. I'm Erica. I've already begun to tell my little boy Joaquin about his Aunt Zinnia. I've heard some of you call her that. I'm one of those who married the culprit. We love each other and there never was any problem about us getting married except the whole time I was carrying our boy his dad was in Iraq. When he shipped out he didn't know - ha! neither of us knew I was expecting. So I dropped out of school - the whole big show - it wouldn't have been such a big deal if he had been home. As it was, I was very a-l-o-n-e. Maybe we are eating for two but believe me, you all know this, being pregnant can be a very singular experience. Just me. All by myself. I saw that ad in the paper that says, 'Pregnant? All alone?' Nailed. That was me. So I came here. I called the number and was given this address. I didn't make an appointment; I just showed up the next day after I called. Big Sis was here. You remember that? She opened the door, nodded her head, took my arm and said for me to come in. Right, just like you're nodding now. I told her my name and started an explanation and she just said, 'I know.' I said, 'But ...' and she said, 'Yeah, I know. Would you like a coke or something?' And it just flooded over me, she really does know. Later I had that same feeling with Aunt Zinnia."

Albuquerque Journal
August 12, 2015
NM Court of Appeals Reverses 'Aid in
Dying' Approval
by Scott Sandlin

A divided New Mexico Court of
Appeals on Tuesday reversed a court ruling
that allowed mentally competent, terminally
ill patients to choose their own time to die
with aid from a physician.

But the 144 pages in three separate
opinions on "aid in dying" - as distinguished
from "assisted suicide" - virtually guarantee,
or at least invite, the issue to be revisited by
the New Mexico Supreme Court, which
chooses the cases it will hear. ...

Chapter Twenty-two

Sally Ingersoll looked up from her desk to see Lance Carroll standing in her doorway.

"Come in Lance. Have a seat." After he had done so she laughed, "If we keep meeting like this, people are going to talk."

He laughed with her and said, "That's exactly why I'm here: people talking. But," he threw up his hands at the look on her face, "not about us."

"Oh?"

"I'd like to float a few ideas before you and then, I don't know, maybe I'll just ride off into the sunset."

"Ideas are welcome."

Lance smiled and leaned forward. "Old people die here: that's your business. It's to be expected and no one questions that - unless for some reason someone does question a death. Now I will not flatter myself that I am saying anything you don't know. I'm just rummaging around in my mental attic. We both know assisted suicide isn't good for hospice programs; it isn't good for Mi Casa. One might learn to use better terminology. One might decide to speak of accompanying someone through death rather than assisting her death. However I believe that resolving that question doesn't change anything. There may be some value in sprucing up the nomenclature. But what does it change? Old people die here. That's your business. We may or may not need a change in words, but we do need a lessening of careless words."

A deep silence filled the room.

Sally stood and walked around her desk. Extending her hand she said, "You're always welcome here, Reverend Carroll."

"Thanks for your time Ms. Ingersoll."

Lance walked through the house looking for family members. He knew Willow wasn't home yet because her car was not in the garage. Through the sliding glass door he saw Zach and Gayle kicking a soccer ball. They seemed to enjoy the sport. Lance couldn't understand it himself. Soccer was not part of his childhood and, although it picked up some interest in recent years as team USA made some headway in the world cup, he couldn't see it. But, if that's what his kids wanted to do, so be it.

He walked into the backyard to watch.

"Hey Dad," greeted Zach. "Come play."

"Not in this lifetime."

"Guess what," Gayle walked over to him and gave him a quick hug.

"You've been invited to perform on New Mexico's Got Talent."

She swatted his sleeve. "No, and there isn't any such show."

"Well, if there were ..."

"Yeah, right. No, I've got news from Nancy."

Lance sat in a patio chair and gestured for Gayle to sit by him.

"She met with a group of girls at the Ladies House and really was impressed with what they had to say."

"Ah-ha. Sounds good."

"I think so. At first she really felt weighed down with the stories she got about dropping out of school and getting a job as a single mom. She's pretty sure she's going to drop out of school but not the working-single-mom bit. The more she heard, the more she felt like, you know, 'I'm not ready for this.' "

"Uh-oh."

"Yeah. She told me she hadn't really realized how much she would have to give up. And she also realized, listening to the others talk, she's not mature enough to be a mother."

"And so?"

"Right now she's thinking the best for her and for the baby is to allow someone to adopt it ... him/her, whatever."

"Do you think she'll stick with that?"

"Oh, I don't know. But I'm thinking that she is starting to be more clear-headed. Yeah, she probably will go with that decision."

After Lance left, Sally sat looking at the chair where he had been sitting. Finally she picked up her phone and called the receptionist desk to ask Lucinda to come to her office.

Lucinda entered Ingersoll's office and, responding to her boss's gesture, took a seat in front of her desk.

"Lucinda, you are aware, I'm sure, that when we tidied up Ms. Foster's room there was no empty pill bottle found anywhere in the room."

The receptionist pressed the palms of her hands together in her lap.

"Yes, I know that."

"I know that day after day you help us care for our clients here. You play an important part in our ministry to precious people."

Lucinda nodded.

"Well I have asked you back here to solicit your help."

This prompted raised eyebrows.

Sally continued, "I would like for you to be an example to the rest of the staff of how we can come together as a team to think about those who live here as our present responsibility and those who will follow them. We need a role model of a positive attitude. Can you do that for me?"

Up to that moment Lucinda had felt a tightness around her heart. She wore a blank expression, sat straight in the chair with her hands in her lap and legs lightly crossed at the ankles. Now, for a second she relaxed back in the chair and then leaned forward, a broad smile crossed her face.

"Oh, yes, Sally, you can count on me."

The next time Lucinda had her hair done Alistair asked about the suspicious death at Mi Casa. Lucinda just laughed.

"That's old news," she told him. "Let me tell you about the affair between Chester Reyes and Maxine Vander Gross."

Zinnia's Girls Memorial Service at the Ladies of Charity House

In the right setting a person might reveal surprising things about herself. The last speaker illustrates the point.

"Samantha here. It's been a year now since I gave my baby back to God. I had no right to rush into bein' a mother and I didn't know what to do about it. Aunt Zinnia - Thank you Erica, I like that - Aunt Zinnia helped me come to that way of talkin' about what I did. I don't know Suzanna. I can see what you're sayin', but I don't see no happy ending yet. Some of you found ways I couldn't see for myself. I had to do this my way. Miss Zinnia, uh Aunt Zinnia, tried to help me decide to give up my baby for adoption. There was no way I could keep a baby. Right now I can't see myself as ever being a mother, but who knows. What we did was wrong. He couldn't see it that way but it was. That made it all the harder on me. God has some pretty clear rules about these things. Miss Zinnia understood how important it is for me to get my life right with God. So, this probably don't make no sense to nobody else, but it makes sense to

me. I couldn't go no other way so Miss
Zinnia helped me come to this. God has that
little soul waitin' to be born and I let him
have that baby back to put into some other
mother. I told Miss Zinnia that baby needs
to go to some more deservin' mother. She
told me to say 'some other mother.' Don't
say 'more deservin' mother.' I'm not there
yet. But I heard her tell me that. And, yeah, I
felt her hugs. I feel them now. I hope when
she breathed her last she felt all of us
hugging her."

Chapter Twenty-three

Willow went about her house cleaning while Lance retired to his study to finish writing his sermon. Usually by this time in the week he had finished the study, research, and analysis of the scriptural text and the topic he had chosen. Now all that remained was organizing his ideas typing them into the computer. This week hadn't gone so smoothly. For some reason, maybe the rogue coming out, he had chosen to find a lesson in Judas' treachery. He thought he wanted to attack the arrogance that would lead a member of a fellowship such as the apostles were to challenge his leader. Why had Judas betrayed Jesus? Maybe it was disbelief. He finally realized he just didn't believe the message Jesus delivered. Maybe it was fear. Perhaps Judas recognized the animosity Jesus had stirred up among the authorities and Judas decided he had better side with those who had the power to destroy them. Maybe it was simple hubris. It could be Judas thought Jesus had taken a wrong turn and Judas meant to stimulate a return to a campaign for political revolution.

"I just don't know," Lance said out loud.

"What don't you know?" Willow had been moving from room to room with a dust cloth and was in the hall when Lance complained.

Lance turned toward the door. "I don't know why Judas betrayed Jesus. Was he a heretic, a coward, an egotist, or a fool?"

Willow threw her hands up. "Men! Who says he has to be any of those? Who wrote the gospels anyway? The men who survived, that's who. The survivors always tell unflattering stories about those who didn't survive."

"Wow! Talk about heresy! It's a good thing women didn't write the New Testament."

"Oh yeah! I heard someone say that Priscilla may have written Hebrews."

"Yeah, I'm the one who said that." After a pause he muttered, "Who says? Who says? Good question." Then Lance turned back to his desk muttering something about finding an old sermon that would do. Instead of opening his sermon file drawer he gazed into the corner of the room.

"Who says?" muttered Zach. He had overhead that last bit of conversation while trotting to the kitchen to find a snack.

"Who says? Who says? That is a good question."

Turning toward the hallway leading to the bedrooms he yelled, "Hey Gayle! Get out here!"

Willow stuck her head out of the study to say, "Zach! really!"

"Well I need to discuss something important with her."

"How important?" asked Gayle from the hall.

"Important enough for you to get your butt in here."

Gayle stomped into the kitchen leading with an index finger pointed at Zach's nose. Zach, naturally, bit her finger - playfully. She wiped her finger on her capris.

"So - what?"

"Who says?"

"Huh?"

"That's a good question. Dad just said so. We go to school and say to everyone, 'Who says Deloit is a goof-off? He's our friend and needs our support and help.'"

"Uh-huh."

"Okay, this is a great idea. That's my contribution. Now you come up with something."

"Come up with what?"

"Well, first we have to change everyone's perspective on Deloit. We do that with 'Who says he's no good?' and then we have to help him. What do we do to help him?"

"I don't know how we can help him."

"All right! I came up with the great original idea, the starting point of this rescue operation. The least you can do is have a simple suggestion, a helping idea."

"Original? You just said Dad had the good question."

"Yes, he did. He just didn't know what he was talking about."

"Ah, like all his good ideas."

"Uh-huh. So how do we help Deloit?"

"He told us: find one or two hundred dollars lying around."

"Sure!" Zach spun around. "That's a great idea. First we 'Who says' 'em, then we organize a fund-raiser."

"Not a car wash; not a bake sale."

"No, it'll have to be better than that. But we are on the way."

302

They high-fived and Zach grinned, "Good job, little sis."

"Are you taking a nap? That's no way to prepare a sermon." Willow stood crossed-arms in the doorway.

He smiled, "Gone to Carolina in my mind."

Willow turned down the hall. "Done that myself a lot lately," she muttered to herself. In the kitchen she almost tripped over Frank. "Watch it guy," she spluttered. She reached down for a quick, reassuring pat on the wiener dog's head. "You can almost be invisible, you know." Her comment caused Willow to jerk up and stare out the kitchen window. A memory was stirred. Someone, who was it - maybe Kathy the young nurse - was musing about the mystery of the missing pills. "It's almost like some invisible person swooped them up." Willow had scoffed, "There's no such thing as an invisible person." Kathy, if that's who the other person was, laughed. "Of course there are invisible people - waiters, maids, even nurses can be invisible. We do our work and people pay no attention to us. Who would be invisible in a nursing home? Lots of people." Who indeed?

Willow mused, who would be invisible enough to spirit away an empty pill bottle? I am, she thought. Sure, nurses can be invisible, but Jennifer is not. She is too obviously present in this story. She could not be the one who could have or would have assisted Zinnia in the pursuit of the good death. And really none of the MCSC staff could have been the one. Who could it possibly be?

"You're deep in thought."

"Oh, Lance. You startled me."

"Sorry. Didn't mean to scare you."

"I'm just ... never mind. Not important."

Chapter Twenty-four

Willow came into the kitchen from the bedroom where she had been reorganizing her closet. Finding Gayle making room in the dishwasher for her glass she said, "I heard the front door slam a moment ago, was that Zach?"

"Yeah. He's gone to find Deloit so he can unload his brilliant proposal."

"What sort of proposal?"

"Oh, he wants to set up a fund raiser to help Deloit and his dad get through a family financial crisis."

"My goodness! How did we come up with such do-gooder children?"

"It's in the DNA - from Dad's side." Gayle laughed.

Lance emerged from the study to catch up with the conversation.

"Are you accusing me of something?"

"We're telling secrets, Dad. You can't come in here."

"No, no," he shook a finger at his daughter. "No secrets in this family."

"Yeah, right! Secrets in this family are the reason I learned how to spell so early. I was well motivated."

Willow leaned back against the refrigerator. "Everyone has secrets of some size," she said. "That's just natural. It's the way of life."

"Even you, Mom?" Gayle feigned incredulity.

"Well, not so much. I'd say I'm the most open one of the four of us."

Lance nodded. "That's true. I would agree."

"Now your father here is a brooding sort who keeps a lot of things to himself."

"Yeah, I know. Why is that, Dad?"

"He has to," Willow decided to answer for Lance. "A pastor has to keep confidences. It's a professional responsibility."

Just at that point Frankfurter waddled into the kitchen from wherever he had been hiding. He looked up at Lance and then at the sliding door to the backyard.

"I would say," said Lance, "that of the five of us, Willow, you're the second most open. Someone here is easier to read than you. Need to go outside, boy?"

Zach was certain that Deloit would welcome the genius-ocity (as he called it) of his plan but that didn't turn out to be the case. He found Deloit at his home late in the evening and attempted a dramatic explanation of his combination repackaging of Deloit's reputation and fund-raising effort. "We haven't decided on the best fund-raising idea yet, but ..."

"Thanks, but no thanks."

"No, really we can ... whadayamean 'no thanks.' "

"Look, Zach, I appreciate the effort but I really don't need it."

"Oh yeah, I think you do. People have a bad image of you in their minds and that's not right. And, besides, you told us some extra money would be a good idea."

"Right. I said that. But it's not true. Well, it's less true."

"What's that s'posed to mean?"

Deloit had invited Zach in and they had gone to Deloit's room to be away from his father. Zach sat in a chair at Deloit's desk and Deloit had plopped onto his bed, leaning against the headboard.

"Well," Deloit said, "I've quit all my part-time scrounging jobs and I'm working full-time at Auto Zone."

"Are you making enough to support you and your dad?"

"Not completely. But it looks like he can get work through a program that manages things like that for people with a criminal record."

"Won't he have to go to jail?"

"We don't think so. First offense, probation, community service - that sort of thing."

Zach looked at him skeptically.

"We'll survive, Zach. This is a rough patch, but we'll survive."

"But still ..."

"We'll survive."

"I dunno."

"I don't want my dad to have a record or have difficulty finding work, but sometimes you have to face up to the consequences. There's no fairy tale happy ending here, Zach, but sometimes just surviving is the happiest ending possible."

"What about your reputation at school? Surely you want us to work on changing minds about you?"

"Ah, not really. My friends, and there aren't many of them, will remain my friends. Everyone else will forget about me. Who needs them?"

Zach quit trying to argue with Deloit. He ran out of arguments, actually. Deloit seemed to have a better handle on his life than Zach had expected.

"I really do appreciate the energy you've put into this idea, Zach. I just don't need to be rescued."

"I can see that."

"How long has it been since your pain meds?"

Lance leaned over Zinnia, mopping the sweat off her brow. Her jaw clamped shut; she leaked tears down the side of her face.

"Minutes before you came," she gasped.

"It's bad, isn't it?"

"It'll ease off ... minutes."

"I wish I could do something for you."

"Talk about it."

"Sure. Whatever you want to talk about."

"Minute."

"Right. Can I get you some ice? Would that help?"

She shook her head. Lance sat back in his chair allowing Zinnia to squeeze his hand. The light began to dim in the room so he reached over to a small table lamp and turned it on. He noted that the warm, homey glow lied about the extreme discomfort in the room. Gradually she relaxed her grip on his hand.

"Any better?"

"Not much but I believe I will be able to talk in whole sentences."

"That's good."

"Short ones anyway."

He patted her shoulder. "Okay, teach," it was a title, not a verb. "What do you have to tell me?"

"Everybody worries about my pain."

"We really don't like for you to hurt."

" 'Preciate it. Pain's not a good thing."

Lance started to respond but Zinnia moved her hand - just enough that he knew she was waving him off.

"Pain hurts, but that's all it does."

He raised his eyebrows.

"There are worse things."

Lance nodded.

"Vomiting, for one thing. I hate that. And there are other things." She looked away. "You don't need to know."

She turned back to him and looked into his eyes. "I need to ask someone a favor."

He returned her look with the same intensity. Finally he nodded.

Acknowledgments

I particularly want to express gratitude to Jennie Rainwater and Kay Hines for sharing insights gathered from their work with pregnant teens.

Suggestions have come from various people. Significant editing was provided by Justin Daniels.

About the author

Jerry M. Self is a native of Wichita Kansas. He has settled for a time in Texas and Tennessee and now lives with his wife Maralee in Albuquerque New Mexico.

Also by Jerry M. Self

Available soon! Read the opening of the next novel in the *WHO-3* series:

Who Knows How We Are Made?

Arrival of the Deputies

The whoosh of the emergency room doors pulled the receptionist's eyes to the sheriff's deputies. Alex Smith, "Smitty," and Aleta Diaz sought a victim. The receptionist directed them down the hall where they could talk to attending nurse Carroll. The nurse informed them that the victim causing her call to the police was undergoing surgery. She described his wounds and then asked them in turn what they had learned from the emergency medical tech.

"Not much," answered Smitty.

"A little more from the guy you told us called for the ambulance," added officer Diaz. "We ran by the scene. The sheriff is out there now checking it out."

"Who's the runner?" asked Smitty.

"Don't know yet," said the nurse. "I'm going to recheck his clothing. But he had no ID on him at all."

"Not anyone from around here?" asked Diaz.

"I didn't recognize him. His face is badly swollen from a broken nose. A gash in his head had blood all over him. But even after I cleaned his face I couldn't be sure if I'd ever seen him before."

Connie

Any parent would be proud to have a hero for a son. Until you consider the price attached. I hate to hear the phone ring any more. Although, I guess I didn't hear it ring when someone called to announce the end of all that warms and brightens my world. I still see Charles, a slightly stooped, black form silhouetted against the blazing white lights of the den, the simple word, "Mom," abruptly halting the party. His brother, my first-born, in the emergency room. I feel Annie's hands on my back and arm. Twilight enters my soul and darkness follows not far behind and with it all dreams die.

My wonderful son, George, always full of surprises, challenged my dreams for him at every possible turning in his life. I'm sure he felt one step ahead of me, particularly when he announced to Arthur and me that he had signed up with the Navy recruiter in Austin. But I was proud of him then with the same tingly joy I felt when he bragged as a toddler about his "poo in the pot," or the hole-in-one he scored his junior year to help the Caliche Hills High School team win a tournament against their biggest San Antonio rivals, the Northside Caballeros. Everything he did for nineteen years, everything, they all fit my dream nicely even if stretching the seams of the dream.

The Party

Arthur and Connie had discussed a party to celebrate George's high school graduation. When George strode into the den with his coup d'état that college would be postponed and paid for by Uncle Sam, they just expanded the party to include all of George's major life changes.

So Connie's dear friend Marie Alders, the sister she always wanted and her daughter Annie helped her craft the party of the season for George. Not that Caliche Hills has a season, or a shopping center for that matter.

George, who loves his mother dearly but loves to tweak her sometimes, dashed through the decorating for his party, a gray blur in his sweats and out the front door throwing back, "I'll just run five miles. Clear the shower for me in about forty-five minutes." Connie was pleased to see him go. She knew he had plenty of time for a run, a shower and to get into presentable clothes by party time. And he was out from under their feet. Good riddance, she thought, but then what does a mother know?

George wasn't gone ten minutes before Elspeth - George's girlfriend - danced in, eager to engineer some mocking surprise for George. She sailed through the front door in carnival mood.

"I've brought a present for Seaman Thompson," she announced.

"No presents," Connie said. "We told everyone, no presents."

"Oh, this won't upset your rule, Mrs. Thompson. Can I hide this in the hall closet?"

Connie said of course she could and chose not to ask questions about the silver wrapped and royal blue ribboned box.

She then grabbed Marie, anxious for some reassurance.

"I know I'm forgetting something," She told her.

"Nonsense, Connie. Everything is just perfect. All you need are the guests."

"And the guest of honor." Shaking her head, she looked at her watch, hoping

George would not be longer than his allotted forty-five minutes.

"Let's walk through the house," said Annie. She's Connie's port in a storm. Of course Connie loves her guys but living in a house with three men who often behave as if they were three rampaging toddlers - well, a mother would need sweet, calm Annie.

Now Annie marshaled a parade through the house. Holding her mother's hand she led Connie, Marie, and Elspeth into the den. A collage of Navy pictures - metallic hued ships and planes, sailors in white shaded with gray, all against teal seas and skies - placarded a theme in the middle of the room. A baby blue banner across the French doors to the backyard announced in a bold, red hand "Bon Voyage, Seaman Thompson!" From the den they walked into the large kitchen, breakfast area. Yellow, red, green and brown makings for tacos, chalupas, and burritos spread across the bar and the breakfast table. Three large coolers, appropriately navy blue, with various drinks on ice sat against a wall. In the dining room the table was pushed against a wall and a Mexican food buffet awaited the guests. The dining chairs and some folding chairs lined the other walls. A brightly painted piñata and streamers added a festive touch.

Charles, the youngest Thompson, and Arthur met the women in the entry hall. They had been setting out red stakes to indicate a parking area next to the driveway. Penelope, their Yorkshire Terrier, trotted along after Charles.

"Sylvester and Dan are here," said Charles.

Marie took her cue to welcome her husband and son. The Alders, Dan and his parents Marie and Sylvester, usually called Syl, must have Italian blood in their veins, although they've never said so. Their dark coloring and slightly chunky bodies contrast so with the Thompson's slim blondness. When the two families converge you could imagine a meeting of Scandinavian hunters and Mediterranean fishers. Elspeth captured Dan and Charles, pulling them toward the closet. Probably she wanted to whisper secrets about her surprise for the "Seaman." Annie stuck with her mother.

Sylvester asked, "Where's George?"

"Out running," said Connie. "But he should be home any time." She turned to Art. "I really don't understand why he isn't already home. This just isn't like George."

"Oh, he found something he wanted to investigate." Arthur waved his hands in his calm-down-Connie gesture. "You know he sometimes gets distracted. Besides, it hasn't been that long."

"Okay. But I'm telling you, Art, if he's late to his own party, I'll wring his neck."

"Well the important thing," Sylvester said, "is when can we eat?"

"Not till other guests arrive," Marie answered. "But your question really was when can you eat. You don't care about our stomachs."

"Okay, I'll ask a more polite question. What can I do to help?"

Connie left that for Arthur to answer while - because she constantly rearranges things until the last minute - Marie, Annie and Connie toured the house one more time. They pushed the dining table to the end of the wall and then back to the center. Annie tugged on the banner. Marie hummed. Connie picked up everything in the kitchen, den, and dining room and set whatever it was back in the same place. The mantle clock startled her. "Is it ...?"

"Six o'clock," said Marie.

People began arriving. The noise level rose, as did the temperature inside. Connie made a point of moving people onto the back patio and asked Art to turn down the air conditioning. A couple of times she asked Annie or Charles if their brother had returned. Quickly she lost count of how many people asked where the guest of honor was hiding. She was not happy. George had never pulled a stunt like this.